The Ibis Sanction

Terran Armor Corps Book 2

by

Richard Fox

For Ryan

Copyright © 2017 Richard Fox

All rights reserved.

ISBN-13: 978-1096993681

CHAPTER 1

Gideon lay half-buried in the blasted remains of a trench, falling dirt smacking into the ground around him as he struggled out of his early grave. The taste of soil and blood filled his mouth. The smell of Hawaii's volcanic soil and the bark of weapons' fire, battling fighters overhead, and shouting soldiers all melded into a din that shook his soul at a primal level.

He managed to grip a broken hunk of masonry that once served as a trench wall and pulled himself out of the landslide of his collapsed trench.

"Nico?" Gideon looked down one side of

the defenses. The remains of his squad were somewhere in the mélange of black soil and concrete blown apart by a Toth bombing run.

"Nico!" Gideon reached for a chunk of masonry just as a blue-white energy bolt streaked in and exploded against the exposed back wall of the trench just in front of him. The blast kicked him back, peppering his face with embers of burning concrete.

Toth battle ululations echoed over the sound of gun fire as the next wave of attackers emerged from the sandy Hawaiian beach.

He rolled to a stop against a dead soldier sat against the firing stoops, her chin against her chest, an open pressure bandage in one hand, an arm pressed against an eviscerated midsection. Gideon grabbed her gauss rifle and struggled to his feet. The blast had thrown him into a still-standing section of the fortifications. In one direction, the sharp angle of the trenches, behind him was ruin.

The hiss-snap of Toth language sent a blossom of fear through his chest. Claws of a Toth warrior's forward legs gripped the top of the trench just over Gideon's head. The warrior was massive, eight feet tall and covered in crystalline armor. Reeking of the sea, the alien looked down at Gideon and bared shark-teeth from its reptilian snout.

Gideon swung his rifle up and pulled the trigger…and got nothing but a dry click.

"Meat," the Toth hissed and jumped at Gideon, foot claws open wide to seize him and rip him to pieces.

Gideon stood frozen, his mind in shock at the first encounter with the alien species. He jerked backwards, the rush of air from the Toth's swipe caressed his face. He came to a sudden stop against the power-armored body of a Strike Marine. The Marine twisted to one side, putting himself between Gideon and the Toth. Gideon saw legs and feet of several other Marines as he was shoved unceremoniously to the ground.

Gauss fire snapped through the trench and struck the Toth warrior, shattering its armor and splattering yellow blood against the trench wall.

"Die, you lizard-looking son of a bitch!" Standish shouted. The Marine didn't have a helmet on, a detail that stuck out at Gideon as he tried to get back to his feet.

The Toth keened and collapsed to the ground, its tail twitching.

"You alright?" asked the Marine that had pulled Gideon out of danger. Gideon glanced at the name and rank stenciled on the man's armor. Lieutenant Hale.

Gideon pointed back towards the dead Toth with his found weapon and tried to speak.

"Nico…I-I can't find Nico," Gideon stammered.

"I got him, sir," came from behind Hale. The lieutenant handed Gideon off to a Corpsman, who guided him down to a firing stoop. "Look at me." Yarrow held up the palm of his medical gauntlet and light flashed from a ring on the Marine's palm.

"Go find Nico. He's…" Gideon shook his head, clearing away some of the cobwebs, and looked down at the rifle in his hands. The round counter integrated into the back sights blinked on and off. He touched the magazine and found it loose, on the verge of falling out. Slapping the base of the magazine hard, he felt the rifle cycle a round into the chamber.

The fear and confusion melted away and a burning knot of anger ignited inside him as he shrugged off the Corpsman's touch.

"You might be in shock," the Corpsman said. "Need to get you back to a field hospital and—"

"Nico is gone." Gideon wiped blood off his face. "He left us. All of us."

The thunderclap of a larger gauss weapon sounded a steady double beat in the air. A giant of gleaming metal advanced up to the trench, twin barrels of the cannons mounted to one arm burning red with heat.

The armor's helm snapped down and stared at Gideon as Toth energy fire snapped overhead.

"Are you going to fight or are you going to

hide?" Elias asked. The armor stepped over the trench and advanced toward the oncoming enemy.

Gideon grabbed the parapet and hauled himself over the top. Toth warriors lumbered through the broken battlefield, emerging from the ocean waves and seeking cover in the remnants of the forward trenches.

Elias charged forward, flanked by the other two Iron Hearts of his lance; Bodel and another, the one who would become Saint Kallen.

Gideon let off a battle cry and sprinted forward, outpacing the Strike Marines in their power armor for the first few dozen yards through bomb craters and ripped razor wire.

Ahead, a Toth warrior reared up in a blast crater and leveled its energy rifle at Elias.

Gideon fired from the hip, striking the alien in the side. The Toth let off a trill of pain and turned its weapon on Gideon, whose next shot cracked the alien's rifle. It exploded in a flash of blue light a heartbeat later.

The Toth crawled along the rim of the

crater, its armor blackened and arms smoking.

Gideon raised his rifle to his shoulder and fired on the alien, the recoil slowing his momentum as he ran. The Toth spasmed as a shot punched through its helmet and exited the other side in a gout of yellow-gray brain matter.

Gideon slowed to a stop next to the Toth's body and glanced over at the Iron Hearts. Elias crushed the skull of a warrior as Bodel rammed his cannon arm into the chest of another and blew its back out with a single bullet.

Kallen…was looking right at Gideon. She pressed her armor's knuckles against her helm to mimic kissing them, then tapped the same fist against her heart.

For a moment, Gideon felt peace. Then the Toth warrior at his feet grabbed him by the ankle. The last thing Gideon saw was the Toth's fire-blackened claws slicing at his face.

****

Gideon snapped awake. The amniosis fluid of his womb sloshed around him, the abyssal darkness of the pod within his armor lit up in a grid.

The Toth-inflicted scars on his face and chest burned, just as they always did after that dream. He felt his heart pounding, his muscles bunched into knots.

Different, he thought. *It was different this time. Nico…*

"Armor, begin conscious cycle for Lieutenant Gideon," came through his womb and into his auditory system. "Authorization Tagawa, LC-44."

"I'm awake," Gideon sent the *Scipio*'s captain.

"Get your lance prepped," she said. "I think we've found her."

****

Gale winds edged Roland off his descent path through the cloud layer enveloping Nimbus IV.

The deep gray expanse around him darkened to the color of red wine below, and the searing light of the system's star washed out the world over his head as he fell. He activated a small maneuver thruster and shunted over to one side, just beyond the limit of his plotted course.

Inside his armor's womb, floating in the amniosis fluid and connected by an umbilical control cord that plugged into his brain through a plug in the base of his skull, he had no sensation of falling as he plunged down at terminal velocity.

A radio channel opened up from his Dotari lance mate, Cha'ril, who was unseen in the abyss of clouds but still close by.

"Roland, we're almost to the break point and if you—"

Wind slapped against Roland's armor, gently rocking him within his womb. The push left him slightly off the centerline of his course, but still within his path's margin of error.

"Something to add, Cha'ril?" Roland asked.

"Got ten-meter swells on the ocean surface,"

Aignar said, coming up on the lance's channel. "Prep your retros for early stop. Get ready for a drop if Mother Nature proves fickle."

"Confirm break floor adjustment up twenty meters," Gideon said and new telemetry data flashed across the HUD fed into Roland's vision.

Roland activated the jetpack bolted to his armor's back and maneuver thrusters on his legs. He glanced over the power levels, then looked down at the approaching darkness.

"Break in three," Aignar said, "two…one. Go, go, go!"

Roland swung his legs forward slightly and ignited his rockets. Inertia strong enough to snap the neck of a normal human felt like a slight push against his body inside the armored womb, enough that he felt his feet just touch the inside of his control pod. Heat warnings popped up on his HUD, and he felt like he had his back to a burning fire pit.

He fell through the bottom of the cloud layer and found an endless expanse of roiling ocean, nothing but white-capped waves the size of buildings thrashing against each other. He searched for a flat patch of ocean to land in as his airspeed shrank to zero.

"No good options," he said. "Geronimo!"

Roland shut off his jetpack and plummeted toward the water. Hydraulic pistons punched the jetpack away and it went tumbling end over end through the driving rain.

Roland pressed his legs together and crossed his arms over his chest just as he came down on the backside of a wave. He wobbled slightly as he sank into Nimbus IV. His armor's sensors switched spectrums and formed a composite of the undersea world through a mixture of heat and sonar, as it boosted what limited visible light made it through the cloud cover and salt water.

"Sound off," Gideon said.

"Feet wet, fifty meters to the floor," Roland said as an eel the length of a city bus swam below him. Bioluminescent dots shimmered along the eel's flanks. Blood-red coral the size of trees dotted the ocean bottom and schools of fish meandered over lime-green sand.

Roland spread his feet hip-distance apart, hitting the ground with a massive thump. A hammer-headed manta ray scurried away. He sent out a sonar pulse and the location of the rest of his lance mates came up. They'd landed in a neat diamond formation.

"Water pressure's nominal," Cha'ril said. "At least we didn't land in another rip current."

"The *Scipio*'s magnetometer picked up a return to the south," Gideon said. "Move out and stay alert for whales."

A waypoint near the edge of a canyon appeared on Roland's HUD. He turned and started walking, his feet drumming up clouds of dust with each step. Worms rose from the sand and clutched at his armor's shins and knees as he went on.

"I'm surprised Captain Sobieski sent us down for this one," Aignar said. "Magnetic anomaly looks like it's in a trench wall, could just be a vein of exposed iron."

"The size and mass are consistent with the

Cairo," Cha'ril said. "More so than the last five drops."

"Lots of asteroid activity in this system, lots of big lumps of metal on the ocean floor," Aignar said. "Is that why the *Cairo* was even in this system all by herself?"

"She's listed as being here on a survey mission," Roland said.

"Then why did she have an entire company of Path Finders on her crew manifest?" Aignar asked. "Nimbus is a protosystem. Won't be properly habitable for millions of years. Drop a drone to collect data and scoot back into the Crucible gate."

"That the Xaros built a Crucible in this system should tell you something," Cha'ril said. "They left jump gates where there were worlds they could settle or where they found remnants of past civilizations."

Roland's HUD blinked with a hit on his armor's magnetometer, he activated a flood lamp on his helm and marched toward the anomaly. A school of fish the size of basketballs fled from his light while ribbon eels squirmed out of the sand and swam toward him.

"Don't remember anything from the Crucible survey about the Xaros liking water planets," Aignar said. "This is the closest thing the system has as far as an Earth-like environment."

"The outer gas giants have extensive moon ecosystems," the Dotari said.

"Then why—if the *Cairo* was out here snooping for archaeotech with her Path Finders— why say she's on a survey mission? Phoenix sending the *Scipio* with the rest of her corvette squadron isn't how we're supposed to do search and rescue."

Roland stopped next to a coral tree and swept his light up the trunk and to the spiny branches. Tiny polyps on the surface opened and closed, grasping at passing plankton. Red mist flowed from the upper branches, their ends broken along a straight diagonal line.

"Roland, you have something?" Gideon

asked.

"Looks like something cut through this coral. Angle doesn't look natural…continuing to the mag anomaly," he said. Roland walked on, faster now. After a solid week of scanning and searching the planet and the rest of the system for the missing *Cairo*, he finally had a possible lead. As much as he wanted this mission to end, finding the ship down here meant there was little hope of finding the ship's crew alive.

A wire outline appeared on his HUD, covering a patch of ocean floor the size of a hangar door. He walked over, and his foot thumped against something metal. He sank to his knees and brushed a swath of sand up, where it caught the gentle current and flowed away like smoke in the wind.

He felt the metal through his armor's fingertips; the surface was pockmarked like lava rock. Roland pointed the twin gauss cannons mounted to his forearm and cycled the autoloader. He carried no ammunition and the weapon sent a blast of water across the hunk of metal, billowing sand up and away.

The sweep revealed a section of starship hull plating, the remains of a pair of white numerals on the far edge.

"Got something." Roland sent images to the rest of his lance. "Hull number...37? That's the *Breitenfeld*. This can't be right."

"That's an 87," Gideon said. "The *Cairo*'s complete number is 387. Besides, the *Breitenfeld*'s been on some secret mission for months."

"Looks like we found her." Roland lifted up the edge of the hull plate, disturbing a small gaggle of yellow and red fish. Floodlights from the other three suits of armor converged toward him through the gloom of the deep water.

"No. We found a piece, not the ship," Gideon said as he neared. "This has reentry scorching on it, could've been lost in orbit."

Roland swung his lamp toward the direction of the larger object that brought them down in the first place. The seafloor ended abruptly a few dozen yards away, giving way to endless water and darkening depths. He dropped the hull section and hurried over to Cha'ril and Aignar, where they stood along the trench edge.

Below, a scar had been cut across the canyon wall, and resting on a shelf—barely visible to his armor's sensors—was a Terran destroyer, her engines half-ripped from the rest of the hull, leaving decks exposed to the ocean.

His HUD returned an error as it searched for the bottom depth of the trench.

"If she'd crashed any deeper, we'd have to call in the Ruhaald," Aignar said.

"The water pressure at the *Cairo*'s depth is 1100 feet," Cha'ril said. "Eighty-five percent of our armor's rated pressure. We're going down there, correct?" she asked Gideon as he joined them.

"We need to learn more," Gideon said. "Hull's mostly intact. We should be able to recover her data banks at least. Cha'ril, Aignar, check the dorsal life pods. Roland and I will get inside. Hit your floats if you go over the edge or the pressure will crush you into paste long before you hit bottom."

"If there is a bottom," Aignar said.

A rising sound like a foghorn reverberated through the water.

Roland and the others snapped off their floodlights.

"Great…whales." Roland ran along the edge of the trench, keeping pace with Gideon. He looked up at the weak light on the ocean surface. The silhouette of massive creatures passed overhead.

"It really is a mistake to call them whales," Cha'ril said. "Earth whales are mammals. I must say that swimming mammals—which is something of an aberration, according to the most recent galactic survey—are fascinating. But we haven't seen these Nimbus whales give birth to live young or even—"

"No one asked, Cha'ril," Aignar said.

Gideon leapt off the edge and sank toward the ledge bearing the final resting place of the *Cairo*. Roland followed suit, fighting the urge to try to swim. His armor was as buoyant as an anvil and was adept at nothing but sinking in this environment.

"The xenobiological classification is important," Cha'ril said. "It's frustrating enough that so many humans think we Dotari are birds just because of our beaks."

"Don't Dotari lay eggs when they have babies?" Aignar asked.

Gideon growled through the comm channel.

"We will discuss this later," Cha'ril said curtly.

Roland landed on the shelf jutting from the canyon side. His footfalls kicked up a spray of bioluminescent life that sparkled in the dark water. He heard the thump of Cha'ril and Aignar landing on the hull of the *Cairo*. The ship loomed over him, an artifact of humanity that did not belong on this world.

"Tell me what you see," Gideon said.

"Scorch marks across the hull." Roland zoomed in on the hull with his optics, recording images and keeping pictures up for comparison.

"Worse on the dorsal. She hit atmo without her shields, then lost altitude control."

He examined the rent where the engines had torn away from the hull.

"The break is twisted, sheared away. Must have happened when she hit the water or scraped along the canyon wall," Roland said. He ran his optics up and down the hull, then did a double take over an open tear the length of his armor's leg.

"Can't be…Cha'ril, you reading any radiation from the hull? Any isotopes from a plasma-graphenium interaction?" Roland asked.

"Negative," she said. "We're almost to the life-pod banks."

"Sir…" Roland was about to send the screen capture of the tear through the *Cairo*'s hull when Gideon sent him three images of similar damage, all ringed by silver metal that had cooled along the edges like scar tissue.

"Rail cannons," Gideon said. "She was ambushed."

"By who?" Roland asked. "Vishrakath use

plasma weapons, same as the Naroosha. No one uses rail cannons as extensively as…we do. This can't be right."

"You think your eyes are lying to you?" Gideon pointed to the central passageway in the *Cairo,* her deck plating dangling from the exposed hull like flesh from a severed limb. "Let's get in there and find the computer core."

"Yes, sir." Roland followed his lance commander to the base of the ship and began climbing up the bulkhead frames.

"At the life pods," Aignar said. A grainy image of an open panel and an empty space in the ship's hull came up on Roland's HUD. "Empty. Every last pod on the dorsal port evac point is gone."

"Same with the starboard pods," Cha'ril said. "Given the burn marks within the pod bay, I'm positive the ship was evacuated *before* she entered the atmosphere."

"Pods are all loaded with mayday boxes," Roland said as he pulled himself up another deck.

"Should've picked them up if they crashed into the ocean...unless they'd all been destroyed before they hit atmo."

Gideon vaulted up into the central passageway and turned his floodlight on as Roland came up behind him. Broken pieces of bulkheads floated in the water, and Roland made out half-open doors and more detritus ahead of them.

"Meet us at server room three," Gideon said, "should. "Should be on this deck."

The foghorn of whale song carried through the ship like a tremor. The *Cairo* canted to one side and Roland grabbed on to the bulkhead out of instinct.

"Why do they think we're food?" Roland asked.

"We did see them tearing apart those jellyfish that were lit up like Christmas trees." Gideon said, snapping off his lamp. "Come, we should be close."

They made their way deeper into the ship, their way lit by their infrared cameras, when a shadow reached out at them from the dark.

Gideon grabbed it and gently swung the loose mass toward Roland. It was a Terran sailor—what was left of him at least. The skin beneath the cracked faceplate was gray and loose, eyes missing.

"Check for tags," Gideon said.

Roland pinched the body's shoulder, the flesh crumpling beneath his armored fingers. His armor's right forefinger snapped open at the knuckle and he scanned the corpse. A small pill-sized object pulsed on his HUD in the center of the sailor's suit.

"Got it. Spacer Apprentice Hellerman, Joseph H. Identity logged." Roland tapped the knuckles of his fist against his helm where its mouth would be, then against his chest twice. He pressed the body to the deck and against the bulkhead. "Sir…he's in his shipboard utilities, not his void combat suit. It takes seventy-five seconds for a graduate from basic training to switch uniforms. He at least had his emergency helm on…doubt he knew much more than the ship was under attack before he died."

"Fits that they were ambushed," Gideon said.

"They knew exactly where to hit her," Cha'ril said as she and Aignar came up behind them. "From what we saw up top, every main power line was severed by rail cannon fire. I doubt the *Cairo* managed to fire back."

"Roland, here." Gideon pressed his fingertips into the seam of a door and bent the reinforced doors open just enough for Roland to stick his helm inside. Stacks of servers within metal housing were bolted to the bulkhead of the small room. One server sat tilted, its corner denting the unit next to it.

"Core's...not looking good. No ambient power. Let me hook up." Roland brought his right forearm into the room. He unlocked a pair of probes from a small hatch on his armor and extended the probes out to the main computer terminal. The probes wavered up and down like cavorting eels.

"Problem?" Gideon asked.

"I've trained for moving the probes around in normal atmo and vacuum…not cold saltwater," Roland said.

"Move." Cha'ril said, nudging his foot.

"I've got…I've got it." Roland plugged both probes into the terminal and the system powered up for a split second, then died with a snap. "Slagged." Roland pulled his probes back into his arm. "Captain must have hit the panic button when the ship was attacked. Even if we pull the units off the wall, intelligence will never recover anything. Even the buffer was nothing but static."

"Wait…buffers," Aignar said. "*Cairo*'s a *Geneva*-class ship. Their point defense turrets have the same optics we do." He tapped his helm. "Six-hour local storage. Won't do a data transfer until a ship stands down from battle stations, keeps the load off the processors."

"Then we find a turret," Gideon said.

"Firing position Bravo-two-eight is at the end of this corridor," Cha'ril said as her three lance mates turned to look at her. "I memorized the ship's schematics. Didn't you?"

The thrum of whale song reverberated through the ship and the deck rocked slightly beneath Roland's feet.

"Moving." Roland strode down the passageway, gripping the deck with the mag plates in the soles of his massive feet. The thump of the Iron Dragoons' footfalls seemed to antagonize the whales outside the ship, and their song filled with clicks.

Aignar sent a brief video clip of a shadow moving against the severed opening behind them.

"At least they're too big to join us in here," he said.

"Isn't there some ancient human hero you can pray to?" Cha'ril asked. "What was his name? Sea Man? He could talk to fish."

Roland slowed to a stop at a round, heavily reinforced door. It was half-open, rolled into the scorched metal bulkhead for the ship's outer hull. He got his helm and shoulders into the turret. The dark void of the ocean pressed through the transparent turret walls. The two gauss cannons extending from weapon housings through the turret on either side of the gunner's seat bore green ribbons of Nimbus sea life.

"You've enough space?" Aignar asked.

"Almost." Roland tried to inch forward, but his ascension kit on his back kept him from going any farther. "The manual controls still hooked up?"

There was a squeal of metal and the hatch widened enough for him to enter the cramped confines of the turret.

A body lay strapped in the gunner's seat. Another sailor in his shipboard utilities. Roland ran his scanner over the dead man, searching for his identity implant. The man's chest was a ruined mess. Broken ribs poked through his uniform, and a leg was bent and broken, a crater of black flesh in the thigh.

"Sir…he's been shot," Roland said. "Close-range gauss fire…got his ID chip."

"Ambushed then boarded. Pull the buffer so we can get the hell out of here. Should be under the gunner's seat," Gideon said.

Roland hooked a finger beneath a handle at the base of the seat and tugged. The seat rocked back and forth as the hydraulics beneath the turret failed to activate.

The rumble of whale song sounded so loudly that he felt his womb quiver in resonance. He looked up and a deep shadow blocked the view from the turret. He activated his floodlight and stared into the massive eye of a Nimbus whale. A yellow iris contracted around a blood-red pupil and the whale reeled back, emanating clicks that sounded like bones breaking in the jaws of a wolf.

"You think you scared it away or just pissed it off?" Aignar asked.

The *Cairo* rocked from side to side as the pod of whales hit it with their tails.

"You pissed them all off. Bravo," Aignar said.

Roland cut off his floodlight, then gently touched the dead sailor's shoulder.

"Forgive me." Roland grabbed the base of

the gunner's chair, ripping it away from the deck. He dug his fingertips into the seam of the hydraulic housing and pulled the machinery that maneuvered the cannons up into the turret. He ripped away pipes and found a bright yellow box.

The *Cairo* lurched to one side, then an unceasing grinding sound—the hull scraping against the shelf—filled the ship.

"We're loose!" Gideon shouted.

Roland stuck the yellow box into a housing on his forearm as the grinding stopped and the ship tipped over into the trench. The hull bashed against the canyon wall and slid lower. Roland braced himself against the turret walls as the ship came to a sudden stop.

"Did the engines get hooked on something?" Cha'ril said.

Roland looked down and into the crushing depths.

"We'll climb back up," Gideon said. "I can see—"

The forward hull of the *Cairo* ripped free

with a screech of metal and plunged down.

Pressure warnings flashed amber on Roland's HUD. A rock outcropping loomed out of the darkness and struck the side of the ship, knocking it into a slow spin.

Roland lifted his right leg and jammed the heel against the glass. The anchor spike meant to keep him grounded when he fired his rail cannons broke through the turret shell and sent cracks through the entire surface. The cracks deepened as the outer water pressure grew stronger by the second.

He swore his womb was tighter as he kicked the glass and shattered it into a million pieces.

"Got a way out!" Roland knocked away the turret frame and sent the gunner seat and cannons spinning into the abyss. He reached down and grabbed Aignar's hand as he reached through the half-open door and flung his lance mate up.

Aignar activated the ascension pack on his armor and hydro-jets unfolded from their housings, shooting him straight up. The back blast hit Roland hard enough that it staggered him against the side of the turret.

Roland pulled Cha'ril free and sent her after Aignar.

His HUD flashed red as the water pressure neared his armor's survival threshold.

"Get out of here," Gideon said as he struggled through the meager opening between the hull and the turret.

"We all go home or nobody goes home, sir," Roland grabbed his lance commander by the armpits and hurled him toward the surface.

He tried to touch the ascension kit's activation switch, but his shoulder actuators ground to a snail's pace as the pressure squeezed against him like a vise.

"*Sancti spiritus adsit nobis gratia.*" His fingers brushed the activation button and the hydro-jets sent him hurtling away from the *Cairo*.

The pressure warnings vanished as he ascended. The dull crump of the *Cairo* succumbing to the depths trailed him like distant thunder.

"I sent the recall buoy to the *Scipio*," Cha'ril said, her voice tinny and weak through the interference of the saltwater. "I'm first to go feet dry. I'll relay telemetry data for the static line pickup."

Whale song pulsed around Roland and his HUD flashed as the creature's sonar bounced off his armor.

"Anyone else getting sick of these things?" Roland asked.

"Keep your speed up," Gideon said. "You miss your burn height and it's a long wait for the *Scipio* to come back."

"You screw up one time..." Aignar said.

Light from the ocean surface grew as Roland ascended, his hydro-jets still churning away. The twinkle of distant bioluminescent creatures appeared in the distance.

"Roland, check your three o'clock," Gideon said. "Think I saw—" His transmission washed out in static as a pulse of sonar hit Roland's armor.

He twisted around...and saw a whale

swimming right for him. A dazzling light rippled down the creature's skin, meant to confuse prey just before the creature struck. Inky black tentacles tipped with hooked teeth the length of daggers reached for Roland.

Roland pulsed his hydro-jets and the tentacles swiped just over his head. The whale kept coming, its jaws open like petals of a flower, alabaster teeth glinting in the light. Roland raised a fist behind his head and punched the whale square in the nose.

There was a crack of bone as the whale compressed against his fist, its forward momentum canceled by the blow. The whale hung in the water, blood seeping from its blowhole, then sank away.

Roland looked up at the sunlight playing across the surface, Roland tilted his helm back, then locked his legs together and arms against his flanks. He burst out of the water and jettisoned the hydro-jets. His jetpack flared to life, sending him skyward on a gout of flame and steam from boiled ocean water.

Telemetry data from the *Scipio* and his lance mates flooded his HUD, and he activated his recovery line. A balloon inflated from a housing on his armor's waist and pulled a reinforced graphenium line skyward as his jetpack slowed his ascent.

Within seconds, the *Scipio* emerged from the clouds and roared overhead. Catch arms along the bottom of the corvette's hull trapped his recovery line and jerked him aside with enough force that it would have killed an unarmored human instantly.

Roland and the rest of the Iron Dragoons trailed from the ship like pennants as it angled to the void and reeled them into the ship's open cargo bay.

"This is Lieutenant Commander Tagawa," the *Scipio's* captain said. "What news?"

"*Cairo* found. Total loss," Gideon said.

"God damn it," Tagawa said. "At least we found them."

"We are armor," Gideon said. "We do not fail."

CHAPTER 2

Roland scrubbed a towel against his head before trading it to a technician for a set of overalls and a pair of boots. He stood on a raised platform connected to the maintenance bay for his armor, its torso open to the *Scipio*'s bay.

"Roland," Gideon called out from the hatch to a turret along the upper levels of the bay. The lieutenant locked eyes with Roland, then ducked into the turret.

"You think any of the *Cairo*'s crew made it out?" asked the tech, a Brazilian man in his mid-fifties named Henrique.

"Looks that way. Where they are now is the

hard question." Roland lifted his right arm up and looked at his forearm, then back to his unresponsive armor. "Damn it. Should've got the buffer box before I dismounted."

"I'll get it." Henrique took a data slate from a hip pocket and began tapping.

Roland stepped into his coveralls, the feel of the fabric almost odd against his skin. Being plugged into the armor for days and weeks on end conditioned his nervous system to be nothing but the armor, to be one with the war machine's systems and the fifteen feet of metal. Every time he left the womb, he felt…lesser.

He stepped into his boots, which he tightened against his legs with leather straps instead of laces. The "tanker boots" were an old tradition, carried down from the American military's original armor corps created by the legendary George S. Patton in the early twentieth century. Roland shifted his weight against the stiff leather, wishing he'd had some more time to break them in.

General Laran, head of the Terran Armor

Corps, insisted her soldiers wear the tanker boots to "set us apart from the rest of the military," as if the plugs in the base of their skulls weren't enough to mark them in a crowd.

He looked over at Aignar's armor. Roland's lance mate sat on a stool while technicians attached cybernetic hands and forearms to where his arms ended just beneath the elbow. A pair of boots with the rest of his legs sat waiting next to him. Aignar had a towel wrapped around the bottom half of his face, masking his missing jaw.

Aignar was once a Ranger and had been badly injured fighting the Vishrakath on Cygnus II. A rare genetic condition kept him from receiving replacement organs, leaving the Armor Corps as his last avenue for service.

Roland looked away as Aignar picked up a black box that held the rest of his face. Despite their time serving together, fighting side by side, watching Aignar put himself back together still made Roland uncomfortable.

"Here you are, sir." Henrique handed

Roland the yellow buffer box he'd recovered from the *Cairo*. It was moist to the touch and smelled of brine. Roland took it, the sudden weight catching him by surprise and he nearly dropped it.

"You want one of us crunchies to help you?" the tech said with a wink.

"Just need my sea legs back." Roland stuffed the box into a thigh pocket and took the ladder down to the deck. He ran around a cart bearing his armor's rail gun and gauss ammunition, then hurried up a set of stairs leading to the turret where Gideon waited for him.

By the time he got to the top, his chest burned and his legs were aching. Moving in armor was effortless and he was trained to operate the armor without the limitations of something so mundane as muscle strength and oxygen.

He was a bit lightheaded and sweating by the time he reached the turret. Inside, Commander Tagawa squatted next to the gunner's seat, already raised up and its buffer box sitting in a neat pile of fiber-optic cables. Cha'ril and Gideon stood against the bulkhead. Cha'ril's head quills were loose, hanging around her head like strands of hair the thickness of a pencil. She held a water bottle to her beak and bit down on the nozzle before taking a long sip.

Roland fished the box out of his pocket and handed it over to Tagawa.

"Ma'am, don't you have sailors that can do this for you?" Roland asked.

"Better to keep this close hold…just in case." Gideon rubbed a knuckle up and down the scars on one side of his face.

"Damn scuttlebutt." Tagawa picked up an omni-tool. The point reshaped itself into a screwdriver head. "My crew's small enough to know what to keep inside the family, but just large enough that I won't know who to keelhaul if something gets out." She looked at Cha'ril, then to Gideon.

"I am armor," the Dotari said. "I am sworn to obey all lawful orders while assigned to Terran armed forces. If this is a sensitive human matter, I can excuse myself."

"She stays," Gideon said. "She saw enough down there to put the pieces together."

A heavy bang of boots on stairs preceded Aignar's arrival. His face, with the exception of his lower jaw, was flush from the climb. He looked at Gideon, then his brow furrowed with confusion. He flicked the small speaker embedded in the front of his neck.

"—thing doesn't want to…there we go," Aignar said through the speaker.

"Button us up," Gideon said and shifted over. Aignar touched the control panel and the round door rolled shut.

Roland's ears fluttered as the air pressure adjusted. He looked at the empty gunner's seat; the image of the dead sailor made his stomach ball up.

"I scanned his tags. His name was Martins," Roland said. "I hope that box can tell us who killed him."

Tagawa glanced around the hydraulics at the turret dome and the storm-ravaged skies of Nimbus

IV where the *Scipio* was in low orbit. She turned the omni-tool around in her hand and hit the base against the buffer housing.

The dome glass flickered and changed to a star field.

"Turret Bravo-two-eight, manned and active." Martins' voice came through the cramped room's speakers. The star field shifted around, showing the camera footage captured in the buffer box. "What the hell just hit us?" Martins asked.

A HUD came up on the screens along with a blinking error message.

"Gunnery? I don't have a target feed from the bridge or the fore turrets," Martins said. Seconds ticked by before the active channel on the screens changed as Martins tried to reach someone else. "Chief Senova, you there? Where the hell is everyone?"

The screens shook and fizzled. The star field lolled to one side, then began spinning. A gray sliver of Nimbus IV appeared at the edge of the image.

"She lost engines," Tagawa said.

"There were a number of precision hits to the *Cairo*," Cha'ril said.

"Tell me they weren't from rail cannons," Tagawa said.

Cha'ril's beak worked from side to side, a Dotari body language cue Roland had learned meant indecision.

A new object, white and red in color, came into view. Roland kept his eyes on it as it traveled across the screen, moving with the *Cairo*'s out-of-control motion. His throat went dry as he made out the outline of the object. It was a ship…a Terran navy vessel.

The ship passed off the screen and the star field settled into place.

"Finally," Martins said. He cursed several times. "Lost power to the turret. Switching to manual control…who the hell's opening my door? We're still running in atmo. You! Shut the blast door before—"

Roland's shoulders hunched as the snap of

gauss fire silenced Martins.

"Rewind the footage," Gideon said, his tone low.

The screens shifted backwards until the Terran ship came up.

"Stop. Magnify," Gideon said. The ship grew larger, remained pixilated for a moment, then resolved into sharp focus, a black "91" clearly outlined on the lower fore hull.

"A *Leyte Gulf*–class battle cruiser," Cha'ril said. "The Terran navy doesn't use a white-and-red hull coloration. The registration number—"

"It's the *Leyte Gulf*," Tagawa said. "I served on her after the second Xaros invasion."

Roland raised his left arm and reached for the screen incorporated into his forearm sleeve. Aignar's metal fingers wrapped over the screen and he shook his head at Roland.

"It was my understanding that all of that class of battle cruisers were sent to the breakers on Barnard's Star," Cha'ril said, "along with most of the Thirteenth Fleet. Part of the modernization efforts after the Hale Treaty went into effect."

"That's what the public was told." Gideon's face was set as he glared at the ghost ship on the screens. "A key part of the Hale Treaty between Earth and a sizable bloc of the Ember War alliance was that we would give up our procedural-generation technology, that we would retire the technology to create a fully trained, adult human being in a matter of weeks…There were some in the military and government opposed to that aspect of the treaty. Specifically, Marc and Stacey Ibarra."

"But the Ibarras have been away on some science mission…" Roland said, frowning as the pieces fell into place, "…for years. And didn't Phoenix nationalize Ibarra Industries right after the treaty was signed? I was a kid when that happened—had other things to worry about in the orphanage."

"Once the treaty was signed," Gideon said, "the Ibarras stole a number of navy ships and vanished into the Crucible jump-gate network."

"It wasn't just the two of them, was it, sir?"

Aignar asked.

"There were some traitors that escaped with them." Gideon stepped away from the wall and leveled a finger at Roland and the others. "This is all top-secret information. You breathe a word of it to anyone not cleared—and everyone on the *Scipio* that needs to know this information is in this room—and you will lose your armor. General Laran's orders. Write your after-action reports with pen and paper and get them to me in the next two hours."

The lance commander hurried out of the turret.

"Hadn't been a peep from the Ibarras since they escaped." Tagawa pulled the buffer box out from under the gunner's seat and picked up the original part. "Hope was that they'd settled some little corner of the galaxy and would leave well enough alone."

"You didn't know anything about this?" Roland asked Cha'ril, who shook her head. "What will the Dotari do if—no, when—they find out?"

"The Dotari have an alliance with Earth, not the Ibarras," she said.

"The Dotari aren't the problem," Aignar said. "What about the rest of the galaxy? The Vishrakath? The Naroosha? We've had a few spats over territory since the treaty. If they think Earth's cheating, it might mean full-scale war."

"What's one rogue fleet got to do with the treaty?" Roland asked.

"Who do you think came up with the proccie tech, Mr. Shaw?" Tagawa screwed the end of a fiber-optic cable into the hydraulic controls, then scooted away from the under-seat housing. "It was the Ibarras. They ran the entire program. Helped usher in three billion people over the course of two decades. You think they skipped the Sol System without it?"

"If the Vishrakath figure out that the Ibarras still have their proccie tubes at work, they—and most everyone else in the galaxy—will hold Earth responsible," Aignar said.

"What? That's not fair," Roland said. "The

Ibarras are renegades, traitors. How are we responsible?"

"Humanity was the last member to join the Alliance against the Xaros," Cha'ril said. "To be part of the Alliance, a species had to be unified, purposeful. This was the way of things for thousands of years. There are no Vishrakath nation-states. The Naroosha do not have factions. The galaxy won't distinguish between the Ibarras and Earth. I did not think this would happen to humans. You passed through a great filter when the Xaros wiped out the Earth. Ibarra saved a fleet made up of a single culture, '—the West,' I think you call it."

"If you think the West never fought itself, I have some reading to suggest to you," Aignar said. "But what now? Earth declares war on the Ibarras for the *Cairo*?"

"First, we get this evidence back home." Tagawa closed up the hydraulics and tucked the buffer box beneath an arm. "I'm heading to the bridge."

Cha'ril waited for her to leave before saying,

"My father told me serving with humans would be interesting. I don't think this is what he meant."

"Gideon knows more than he's telling us," Aignar said. "I've never seen him so worked up before—not even when we were dealing with the Vishrakath."

"Who wants to ask him?" Roland raised an eyebrow.

Silence.

"Yeah. Neither do I," Roland said.

CHAPTER 3

Roland hefted a duffle bag onto his shoulder and marched down the gangplank extending out of one side of the *Scipio* and to the floor of the hangar beneath Olympus Mons. He looked up to the roof, almost a half mile above his head. Force fields separated the hangar's atmosphere from the thin air and pink skies of Mars beyond the largest mountain in the Solar System.

The sheer scale of the corvette hangar always left him in awe at the engineering prowess that went into the Terran Armor Corps' home base. The entire complex stretched out beneath Olympus—: training areas, underground cities, manufacturing plants…all for the armor and the Martian defenses.

On the *Scipio*'s main ramp, the Iron Dragoons' armor slid down on anti-grav generators within their sealed maintenance pods, their "coffins." With the weight of the bag and the exhaustion of arriving at Mars during the middle of their normal sleep cycle, Roland longed to be back inside his armor.

"Home sweet home," Aignar said from behind Roland.

"You prefer this to Earth?" Cha'ril asked.

"I prefer anywhere I'm not stuffed into a navy can with a bunch of squids that haven't showered in days," Aignar said.

"Serve on a Dotari ship for a few months," Cha'ril said. "You'll find the *Scipio* has plenty of room in comparison."

Gideon waited for them at the base of the ramp. He scrolled through a data slate as the three huddled around him. Drone carts rolled through the hangar. A trio of armor soldiers in red-painted armor emerged from a sally port and strode to another corvette at the opposite end of the hangar.

The iron tang of Martian air hit Roland's nose. Growing up in Phoenix, he was used to a dry heat; the cool, moist air of Olympus tinged with red dust gave the place its own distinct scent.

Roland and the others waited as his lieutenant scrolled down a data slate, then looked up at them.

"Our lance remains on deployment cycle," Gideon said. "Armor's going to tech bay seven for quarterly services. Be there at 1700 local."

Roland's heart sank. He understood the value of being a part of his armor's regular maintenance—his user insight often caught problems the diagnostics did not—but the more he tried to help, the more annoyed the technicians became with his presence.

"The brass want to see me in the Castrum," Gideon said, citing the headquarters structure for all of Olympus. "What we encountered on Nimbus remains quiet, understood?"

"Yes, sir." Roland tapped a data slate in a pocket. "Speaking of, seems all our accounts are locked. If you need to reach us before 1700…"

"Forgot about that—one second." Gideon tapped on his screen and the data slate in Roland's pocket vibrated with new notifications.

"Stay out of trouble." Gideon said, holding up a hand, and an empty cargo sled pulled up next to him.

Roland pulled his data slate out and looked through a month's worth of messages. He scanned down the senders' names, hoping for a note from Jerry, his old friend from the orphanage that joined the Rangers the same time Roland volunteered for the Armor Corps…but all he had were administrative notices from the battalion's adjutant. He didn't bother looking for anything from Masako. He'd given up on her months ago.

"Only three months until we're off deployment cycle," Aignar said. "You still going back to Dotari for leave, Cha'ril?"

She didn't answer. Her eyes fixed on her

screen. Her skin went almost pale blue as the tip of a quill quivered next to the base of her beak.

"Cha'ril?" Aignar asked. "You okay?"

"My leave has been cancelled," she said. "Seems I won't be going home anytime soon."

"That's bullcrap," Aignar said. "Thought the Corps couldn't stop a Dotari from going home at least once or twice a year."

"It was not the Corps…my. My father did it." She adjusted her pack, then slid her slate into a thigh pocket. "I must…excuse me." She summoned a sled and was gone seconds later.

"Nothing's ever easy, is it, kid?" Aignar asked Roland.

"I got nothing special." Roland shook his slate gently. "Just that Dr. Eeks is on planet and needs to do a checkup on my plugs. There's a Templar fellowship on Stack C-31 in half an hour. Want to come?"

"You want to go do that instead of sleep, eat, or take a shower that doesn't have a thirty-second ration time?" Aignar asked.

"The Templar won't let us stand the Vigil unless two inducted members vouch for us. No one will do that unless we go to fellowship and practice." Roland looked down at his bare left chest pocket, where a Templar cross would go once the order accepted him.

"I've been a bit…lacking in my service to Saint Kallen," Aignar said.

"Then let's go." Roland said, holding up a hand. "It'll be fun!"

****

Roland caught a glimpse of the sword as it slashed at his face. He swung up the blade of his own wooden sword and managed a block that bounced the training weapon against the thin metal bars of his helmet.

He didn't see the kick that struck his stomach, but he felt the sting and the whoosh of air out of his lungs. Roland doubled over, and his opponent chopped down on the pads protecting

Roland's neck.

Roland fell to one side, struggling to breathe as his diaphragm failed to function for a half second.

"You haven't been practicing," Lieutenant Tongea said as he removed his helmet and held it against his side. The Maori wiped sweat off his tattooed face and shook his head.

"We…were…" Roland coughed.

"Are you going to offer me an excuse?" Tongea set down his wooden sword and helmet and helped Roland sit up.

"No, sir." Roland took in a deep breath and winced.

"You think this is foolish? Armor practicing with sticks when we carry rail weapons and gauss cannons?" Tongea slid Roland's helmet off to look him square in the eye. "That this is somehow beneath you?"

"No, sir…Can we have another match?"

"You think it will go differently?" Tongea half-smiled at him.

"I'll improve. Bruises are a decent teacher." Roland reached for his weapon but Tongea knocked it away with a flick of his sword tip.

"You may not be ready for this. For the Templar," Tongea said.

"What? I am. I need practice, but it will—" Roland struggled to get up, but Tongea poked him in the chest with his sword and kept him seated.

The Maori sat down next to him and crossed his legs, then rested the sword over his thighs. He tapped the red cross sewn onto his white tunic.

"Why the sword?" Tongea asked. "Why do we bother learning this when we fight with guns and cannons?"

"The first Templar, Colonel Carius, carried one when he fought the Xaros on their home world. Their leadership caste wasn't flesh and blood. The swords were designed to kill the Xaros."

"Not quite," Tongea said. "The sword is a symbol. Carius—and all the Martyrs—took up the Excalibur swords because it was the only weapon that could win victory against the Xaros, to save

Earth and the human race. The sword is our promise, our vow that the Templar will protect humanity at all costs. Not every Templar carries a sword. The Uhlans have their lances. Odinsons their hammers."

"If it's a symbol, why bother practicing?" Roland asked.

"Vows are worthless unless deeds are wedded to them," Tongea said. "If you can't wield the blade, you won't respect what it stands for."

Roland nodded slowly.

"But that's only one part of becoming a Templar." Tongea got back onto his feet. "You want to become part of the order? Wear the cross on your armor and uniform? You must know the hymns, the prayers…then we'll consider letting you stand the Vigil at Memorial Square. You won't be a Templar until then."

"I'm having trouble with the hymns. They're so long. And in Latin," Roland said.

"You are armor. You went through the most arduous training and selection process humanity has for its warriors, and you can't memorize a few dozen pages of Latin?" Tongea grabbed Roland by the forearm and pulled him to his feet.

Around them, pairs of Templar and initiates sparred with wooden long swords on bamboo mats. Tongea pointed across the training area to rows of pews arrayed in front of a shrine to Saint Kallen. Aignar and several others were there, all reading from hymn books.

"Ask Brother Cordeswain to help you with memorization," Tongea said. "The next time you step on the mat with me and you fight below my expectations, I'll give you a good scar to remind you to practice."

"Thank you, sir." Roland winced as he felt the ache of accumulated bruises beneath his armor.

****

The door to Cha'ril's barracks room slid open and she hurled her duffle bag against the far wall, breaking a wrought-iron sculpture of a nest.

She stomped into the room and glared at the door as it slid shut, wishing she could have slammed it.

She paced back and forth, emanating a constant hiss punctuated with clicks from her beak. She tapped her fingertips together, then kicked a low stool into the bent nest sculpture on the floor.

Her barracks managed to make her angrier. The proper Dotari bed made of a bowl-shaped cushion hanging from the ceiling, a mist shower unit, her stash of salted *gar'udda* nuts in her closet—all vivid reminders of her home world that her father had forbidden her from visiting.

She took her data slate out of her uniform and slammed it against the recharging pad built into her desk. A holo screen popped up and a high-priority video message pulsed for her attention. It was from her father, not sent by his military account and with a heavy Dotari encryption that stopped her from listening to it in public.

Cha'ril kicked off the human tanker boots and let her feet splay out. She gripped a stool with overly long, claw-tipped toes and dragged it in front of her desk. She stood on top of it and squatted down, sitting like a proper Dotari and not pressing her hindquarters against things, like the humans always preferred.

She pulled out a small shrink-wrapped bunch of red fruit still attached to a cut branch, hesitated for a moment, then tore open the packaging and popped a raw coffee berry into her mouth. She chewed it quickly and a gentle wave of euphoria passed through her body. Her anger subsided and a dull buzz filled her ears.

The Dotari had first encountered the coffee plant on Hawaii. A few enterprising individuals discovered a recreational effect for the raw fruit, a secret not shared with their human hosts.

Cha'ril pinched another coffee berry between her fingers, then wrapped it up in the plastic and gently returned it to the desk.

"Play message seven-seven-eight," she said.

The holo screen snapped to her father in his office, the skyscrapers of Phoenix in the background.

"My sweet nestling," Un'qu said, "I'm sorry I cannot give you this news in person, but your deployments are difficult to track. I cancelled your trip to Dotari, not out of anger, but to protect you." His forehead deepened in color, a sure sign he was upset.

"The phage has become worse. We thought returning to our home world after the war, after our long exile in the void and on Takeni, would be our salvation. We were no longer the itinerant Dotok, but rightful Dotari, proud of our homes and our nation. But the disease has proven too tough, too resilient to our science.

"Children are dying," he rubbed a tear away from the corner of an eye. "We thought they would be the most resilient to the phage, but their immune system collapses faster than an adult's. The Council of Firsts is on the verge of declaring a quarantine, forbidding any healthy Dotari from setting foot on our world.

"The Terrans are most helpful. They've sent their best doctors and scientists to aid us, but they've had just as much success as we have in developing a treatment. There is a joint…effort underway with the humans. One I can't discuss on this channel. It is a long shot, but as the humans say, 'Cod mittens…Goof missives.' No…"

"*Gott mit uns,*" Cha'ril said. Older Dotari were notoriously bad at speaking any human language but English. The younger generation had developed their tongues to embrace more of their allies' esoteric sayings. But why her father would invoke a human battle cry, even one that famous, didn't make any sense to her.

"Your mother and brothers are still there, still healthy, but I cannot risk letting you go back. If Dotari is lost, along with ninety percent of our population, it could doom our species. As such, the Council of Firsts has ordered the removal of hormone blockers from all Dotari Expedition ships and food processors."

Cha'ril almost choked on her coffee berry.

"Any eggs will be cared for in crèches on Hawaii or Dotari vessels as per our treaty with

Phoenix. That's the official position. As your father…it never occurred to me that you'd ever have children until you transferred back to the Dotari armor brigade and married, yet this is the world we live in. Given your age…the urge will be quite strong. I wish I could do more for you, but at least your mother can still send you videos from home to help you through this. Do come see me when you can."

He signed off with their family trill.

Cha'ril stared at the blank holo screen for a moment, then took the whole pack of coffee berries back out of the desk.

CHAPTER 4

The mess hall servicing the main armor barracks beneath Olympus was a bit of an anachronism; it had a kitchen. The bang of pots and pans against stoves, the sizzle of cooking meat, and a complete omelet station always made Roland think of Earth and his last job as a waiter in a restaurant that went to the great expense of hiring human chefs.

When modern robots could cook food perfectly and a single food printer could deliver tailored nutrition quickly and easily, the nuances that came from others preparing one's food almost felt like a luxury.

Roland set a tray of food next to Aignar,

then inhaled the aroma of his pasta dish. Aignar looked down at his meal inside an enclosed cup and straw, then back at Roland.

"The Andouille sausage smells incredible." Roland jabbed a fork into his meal. "I actually saw them making the pasta back there. I can't believe it."

Aignar stuck a fingertip against his jawline and pressed twice. His prosthetic jaw snapped open slightly, then he maneuvered the straw between his lips and pinched them shut around the straw. He took a long sip of nutrient paste, then set the cup down just hard enough to make a statement.

"Oh," Roland blushed. "I'm an asshole. Aren't I?"

"Not at all. This is my favorite flavor of gloop and I'm not sharing it with you," Aignar said.

Roland took a bite of his dinner. His face contorted in pain a moment later.

"Bit myself again," he said. "Damnedest thing about being in the armor for so long. You forget how to eat. Crap. I did it again."

"You keep making it weird and I'll stop eating with you," Aignar said. "How was your sparring session with old man Tongea?"

"One-sided." Roland took a quick glance around the mess hall. "You ever notice that the Templar, the ones that have stood the Vigil and can wear the cross, never sit with anyone but each other?"

"Probably because they don't waste time speaking while at meals," Aignar said. "They train and they fight. Any time not in armor is time you're losing your synch rating."

"Not like we have much time for socializing," Roland said. "This is our third time back on Mars since the dustup on Barrada almost eight months ago…You know any lances that have Templar and non-Templar armor in them? Seems like every lance is either all Templar or not at all."

"Don't think so. Why do you ask?"

"Lieutenant Gideon. He's never said a word about the Templar. Hasn't shown a speck of interest in them, which strikes me as odd since I heard he must have seen Saint Kallen on Hawaii during the Toth attack. He's got that same fire as the Templar. Why hasn't he ever joined? What's going to happen when we're fully inducted?"

"You think we'll be transferred?" Aignar asked.

"I don't want that. Gideon's taught me so much—I can't imagine following anyone else. And Cha'ril…sure, she's a—oh hi, Cha'ril." Roland scooted over on his bench to make room for her.

The Dotari set a steaming bowl of *gar'udda* nuts down, then sat with her hands balled in her lap. She looked up at Aignar sitting across from her, then leaned to one side. She snuck a peek at a table with three male Dotari armor. One of them nodded to her, and she ducked her head back, using Aignar to block her line of sight.

"Everything okay?" Roland asked.

"Of course it is. Why wouldn't it be?" Cha'ril popped a *gar'udda* into her mouth and cracked it loudly.

Roland cringed.

"Everything okay?" Aignar asked, his tone almost petulant through his throat speaker.

"I cannot enjoy my meal if I have to abide by all your rude table manners." Cha'ril shifted over and sat shoulder to shoulder with Roland. She ate her next nut more gently.

"Cha'ril, what will you do if Roland and I become Templar?" Aignar asked.

"I don't know if anything would change," she said. "Given the passion with which the Templar fight to protect humanity, I thought there would be some open hostility to my alien nature, yet I have never experienced any sort of ill treatment or aggression. Nor has any other Dotari armor voiced a complaint."

"There are two Dotari at Memorial Square," Roland said. "According to High Chaplain Krohe, they had their weapons blessed before the final battle with the Xaros."

"An unusual act for a Dotari," Cha'ril said. "I believe it had more to do with the connection between fallen Caas and Ar'ri and the Iron Hearts than any sort of religious notion. Our spirituality comes through community and our link to our parents and...hatchlings." She dipped her head slightly and focused her attention on her bowl.

Roland glanced at Aignar, who shrugged.

"Special dessert," a low voice rumbled. A hulking figure in chef's whites pushed a trolley with several tiers of small plates between the tables. He had a shock of white hair and skin colored shades of deep green and black in segments almost like a turtle's shell.

"Hello, Cookee," Roland said to the doughboy. "We missed you."

"Portuguese egg tarts." Cookee set down a plate with four bite-sized custard treats with small scorch marks across their yellow tops. He waited for Roland to take a bite and give him a thumbs-up, then reached to a lower tier and brought out a pair of *gar'udda* nuts covered in cinnamon and sugar.

"Churro gar nuts for Dotty friends." The doughboy set the plate in front of Cha'ril, who recoiled slightly.

Roland kicked her under the table.

Cha'ril took a slow, excruciating bite, then nodded at Cookee.

"Thumb. Give him the thumb," Roland muttered.

Cha'ril stuck a thumb out parallel to the table, then rotated it up.

The doughboy grunted and moved on.

"I don't understand why you tolerate that…thing." Cha'ril spat her churro-flavored nut into a napkin.

"What? The egg tarts aren't half-bad. Cookee's getting better." Roland ate another one.

"I still wonder if its underlying programming to kill nonhumans is still at work. What did he do to those poor *gar'udda*? Fry them in some sort of oil then toss them in poison?" Cha'ril asked.

"Let me try." Roland sniffed the fusion of Dotari and Earth cooking and took a small bite. "Not half-bad."

"Barbarism," Cha'ril said.

"He's one of the very last doughboys," Aignar said to Cha'ril. "It won't hurt you to be kind to him."

"It is an *it*, not a *he*," she said. "It is a biological computer in human form designed to fight. I don't understand your affection for them."

"They filled the gaps during the Ember War," Aignar said. "Served as infantry on the ground and counter-borders in the navy, and they died in droves fighting the Xaros. Most reached the end of their service life after the war, but a couple were abnormal, kept ticking. We couldn't just…put them down."

"Something of a human tradition," Roland said. "Prewar militaries used dogs, horses. Their handlers took care of them when their service ended. Cookee found a niche in the kitchen. I heard there's even a doughboy in the Strike Marines."

"That doughboy a genius or the jarheads getting that stupid?" Aignar, the former Ranger who had no love for a sister service, asked. He laughed, the monotone sounds from the speaker in his neck always came through with a mocking tone, no matter the intention behind his laughter.

"Doughboys—another Ibarra Industries innovation," Roland said. "I think there are only a few dozen left. Most were retired from service after the war."

The data slate in his pocket vibrated three times. He let out a sigh.

"Just when I sit down to eat." He removed the device as all conversation in the mess hall died away.

"Deployment orders," Aignar said, reading from his slate.

"Back to the *Scipio*?" Cha'ril asked as she scrolled through her screen.

"No, the *Ardennes,* one of the new battleships," Aignar said. "Wheels up in two hours."

"Roland, you got the same orders?" Cha'ril's brow knit in confusion.

"I do," Roland said. He looked around the room as; tables with human armor soldiers quickly policed up their trays and made for the exits. The

Dotari soldiers watched them go. More than one had their slate out, shaking their heads.

"Here it is," Cha'ril said. "The *Ardennes*, but my orders have amendments from Colonel Martel and Lieutenant Gideon."

"Mission objective and location is restricted," Roland said. "I'm looking at the roster and I don't see any Dotari lances. Why not?"

"You don't bring friends to a family feud," Aignar said. "Time for the Ibarras to answer for what they did to the *Cairo*."

****

"Roland…wake up."

He opened his eyes and dim light grew within his womb. He kept his HUD off but sent an impulse through the umbilical connecting him to his armor. The synch rating between him and the war machine was just over eighty percent efficiency, barely optimal for combat operations.

His armor stood inside a storage pod, a

lidless coffin within the expansive armor ready bay within the *Ardennes*, the cemetery. All the ship's armor idled in the cemetery, the soldiers resting within the suits to increase their bond with the war machine they brought to battle.

"Roland?" Cha'ril asked.

"I'm up," he said. "What's wrong?"

"Nothing's wrong. If something was wrong, I would have spoken to you before your synch rating crossed the combat threshold," she said quickly.

"You've been acting weird."

"No! I just want to…ask you about babies," she said.

Roland stretched his legs out to make sure he wasn't somehow dreaming.

"Not weird at all. You know Aignar has a son. You should probably ask him," Roland said.

"His synch is still amber and he is most agitated when I've woken him up in the past. But since you're awake, I'll ask you. The Ibarras created the procedural-generation technology shortly after the initial Xaros occupation of Earth was defeated. They could create a new human being with tailored skills in days, all unique and with their own set of false memories of a full life up to the moment they were created. Nothing like this had ever existed on Earth. Why did humans incorporate the procedurals so easily into society?"

"If I'd known there would be a quiz, I would have studied," Roland said. "I'm true born, have to be because proccies can't be armor. I was surrounded by true born my entire life until my parents died in the war and then it was off to the orphanage, where the adults taking care of me were probably proccies. Almost everyone over the age of thirty in the Solar System is a proccie. Thing is, I could never tell the difference between true born and proccies."

"But what if you could? If they all had the doughboys' mottled skin, for instance."

"The root of most human conflict is being able to distinguish someone else as an 'other.' Maybe that's why we didn't keep the doughboys in production; they're just too different. Ibarra was smart. He made the proccies so there's no discernable difference between them and a regular human. They have children, who're no different than any other true born. They 'remember' a life that makes up their history. Not everyone was happy to hear about this, but no one seems to care anymore."

"So why give up the proccie tech?" she asked. "It seems to be a major advantage for Earth."

"Ask Ken Hale and the rest of the negotiators," Roland said. "All I remember was some big announcement on the networks and then we had a day off from school to celebrate the treaty every year after that."

"So you don't care if a prospective mate is a proccie? No concern for long-term genetic effects on your descendants?"

"Back to being weird again."

"I can rationalize why Earth embraced proccies. The Xaros returned with tens of billions of attack drones, years before they were expected, and

Earth was nearly lost a second time. That Earth had procedural defenders made the difference between victory and extinction. But for the Dotari…it would have been impossible to accept. Parents form their bond with hatchlings, not while they're gestating in their eggs. That is why adoption is almost unknown within Dotari history. I could get into the hormonal changes…but just know that is the way we are. The idea of a Dotari conjured out of thin air evokes an almost primal hatred from me."

"I don't think there will ever be a procedural Dotari for you to worry about," Roland said. "If they really did rebel over it, I doubt the Ibarras would share the tech with you anyway."

"Likely not. Are you aware of how Dotari mate with each other?"

"Cha'ril, please don't. We've been over this."

"You remain very sensitive to this topic. Humans are not averse to learning how their own species copulates. My survey of your Internet archives—"

"I told you not to open that link Aignar sent you."

"—shows a great interest in the topic of copulation. Along with videos of cats, for some reason. I fail to understand your reticence. Don't human children engage in a ritual entitled 'you show me yours, I'll show you mine'? If you examining my cloaca will enhance our dialogue, then—"

"I do not want to see your cloaca and while we're on this topic—again—stay out of the men's locker room." Roland squirmed inside his womb. "What is really bothering you? You have a bad habit of beating around the bush when we're discussing anything not related to our armor or fighting."

"Humanity came to a decision point during the Ember War. You chose a massive disruption in your culture, to your species, for the sake of survival. If the Dotari had to do the same thing…I'm not sure we could."

"It's not like there was much of a choice.

Ibarra snuck proccies into the fleet, into Phoenix…he even made his own fleet, the Lost 8th that turned the tide when the Toth came knocking. He didn't give the survivors of the first battle with the Xaros an opportunity to even consider the implications. One day we woke up, and the proccies were everywhere and were vital to winning the war."

"Do you hate him for that?"

"How can I? We won the war. The Xaros killed off every sentient species in three-fourths of the galaxy before they got to Earth. I'd rather be alive and have a few moral questions than dead with a pristine conscience. But the *Cairo*…" A shiver went down his back as he remembered the bodies floating deep beneath the sea. "I can hate him. We can find him and Stacey Ibarra and drag them back to Earth for a trial."

A door at the end of the cemetery opened and Gideon walked in. The lieutenant put an earpiece on and joined Roland and Cha'ril on the lance network.

"Iron Dragoons, wake up," Gideon said.

"Huh? Pork chop sandwiches," Aignar spat as his armor roused him from slumber.

"Always ready, sir," Roland said.

"Admiral Lettow wants all armor at the next operations briefing. One hour. Decant and meet me there. Uniform is shipboard utilities," Gideon said.

"Can't we just remote in like we did on the *Scipio*?" Aignar asked. "We'll lose synch and—"

"Did I stutter?" Gideon asked.

"No, sir," Aignar said.

"Should I go to the admiral and tell him this briefing isn't convenient for us?" Gideon asked.

"No, sir. Sorry, sir," Aignar said.

"This isn't the *Scipio*. Big-ship drivers like Admiral Lettow do things their own way and we are guests here. Fifty-eight minutes. Deck three. Do not be late." Gideon pointed a finger at Aignar's armor and stormed out.

"Damn it. I texted Henrique. All the techs are in the middle of a damage-control drill," Aignar said. "Can you two help put Humpty Dumpty back together again?"

"We've got you." Roland activated the dismount protocols for his armor. Expelling the hyper-oxygenated amniosis fluid from his lungs was never pleasant but had become easier with time.

"You don't have to ask," Cha'ril added.

****

The *Ardennes'* briefing room was a small auditorium with dozens of rows rising slightly from a stage with the ship's colors and the Terran Union flag next to a single lectern. The auditorium could have seated well over a hundred but was packed to standing room only.

Roland pushed through a throng of sailors, all with different ship patches from the *Ardennes*, attempting to reach the rows where Gideon's last message told them to meet him. He reached a pair of Rangers in matte-black combat armor blocking the lower rows; each had a gold cord on their shoulders, marking them as the admiral's personal security detachment. The aisle behind the captain was full of more Rangers, their uniforms in stark contrast to the light gray of naval personnel.

"Pardon me," Roland said to a Ranger with captain's bars.

The captain glanced at the warrant officer pip on Roland's uniform and pointed back the way Roland came.

"Primary staff and 14th Fleet captains only, chief," he said. "Beat it."

"Why are you still standing here?" Cha'ril pushed through the press of bodies and looked at Roland. "We have four minutes to be seated."

Roland turned around to face her. "I think the lieutenant might have—"

"Chief, my apologies," said the Ranger captain as he tapped Roland on the shoulder. The Ranger tapped the base of his own skull, where Roland had his plugs. "I didn't recognize you as armor. The admiral has you in the front row."

"Make a hole," the other Ranger said. "Armor coming through."

To Roland's surprise, the Rangers blocking the aisle snapped to the side.

The captain beat his fist against his heart and lowered his head slightly. Roland nodded quickly and hurried down the stairs. The cordon of Rangers, all with the air of hardened killers and service stripes on their forearms, gave him and the rest of his lance plenty of room as they passed. Most repeated the captain's salute.

Roland spied a row of men and women with plugs. Gideon turned around and waved them toward three empty seats, glancing at the clock on his forearm screen as Roland took the seat next to him.

"Two minutes to spare," Gideon said. "Did you get lost?"

"That is correct, sir. This ship is a lot bigger than the *Scipio*," Roland said. Gideon grunted, then turned his head to speak to the lance leader for the Uhlans.

Aignar slipped into the seat next to Roland. He looked down at his metal hands, touching the thumbs to the other fingertips one at a time.

"Aignar, you were a Ranger. What was that salute?" Roland asked.

"I keep forgetting you've never been around anything but armor and the *Skippy,*" Aignar said. "Those Rangers keep to Saint Kallen."

Roland glanced at the Uhlans. Each, as full members of the order, bore the Templar cross as a patch on their uniforms.

"But we're just armor, not Templar," Roland said.

"Doesn't matter to them." Aignar's eyes darted toward Gideon. "I'll explain later."

Curtains across the back of the stage opened, revealing a carved emblem of the *Ardennes*: a boar's head with a single text-bearing ribbon beneath it.

"What does '*Resiste et Mords*' mean?" Cha'ril asked.

"'Resist and bite,'" Roland said.

"Your mouths are like a Dotari baby's—useless in a fight. I don't think I will ever understand you humans," she said.

The room fell silent as Command Master Chief Petty Officer walked onto the stage and stomped his foot into the position of attention.

"Admiral Lettow!" he shouted.

Roland went to attention, eyes locked forward, as the admiral marched onto the stage. Lettow had salt-and-pepper hair and a neatly trimmed beard. He would have had vid-star good looks, were it not for a nose that looked like it had been broken many times and a patch of scar tissue over his left ear.

"Be seated," Lettow said as he stepped behind the lectern. The lights dimmed and a holo field formed next to him, taking up the rest of the stage. The whole of the 14th Fleet, nearly eighty vessels in formation around the *Ardennes,* appeared in the holo. The image zoomed out, showing their course from Mars to the Crucible gate near Ceres, now Earth's second moon after the Xaros relocated the dwarf planet during their occupation of the solar system.

"The 14th is on course for a wormhole jump to the Oricon system," Lettow said. "Eight hours ago, the Crucible detected unauthorized activity at the Oricon gate. The colony managed to get this image through before all contact was lost."

The image changed to a Crucible gate, the massive basalt-colored segments joined together like a crown of thorns, a fleet of Terran vessels emerging from the active wormhole.

"Those are not our ships," Lettow said. "They belong to a rogue faction controlled by Marc and Stacey Ibarra." The admiral waited as the auditorium—with the exception of the armor, all the armor—murmured in disbelief.

Lettow raised a hand, a hand missing three fingers, and silence returned.

"The Ceres Crucible recorded another wormhole activation thirty-nine minutes later and has been unable to access the Oricon gate since then. The Keeper says there's a quantum interference pattern disrupting her attempts to open a new gate, but she'll have the code cracked before we arrive in a few more hours.

"Our mission is to safeguard the Oricon colonists and…" Lettow bit his bottom lip. "…then bring the rogue ships back under Terran Union control. No matter the cost. If this can be done without bloodshed, so much the better. If not…"

"What do the Ibarras want there?" asked one of the fleet captains.

"Intelligence hasn't given me a good answer to that," Lettow said. "Oricon is a silver-tier colony still under construction. One main settlement with a few engineer outposts. No more than a hundred thousand souls. That Oricon is a moon orbiting a gas giant is the only thing of note."

The admiral tapped the lectern and the holo changed to an organization chart of the 13th Fleet with a few ships grayed out. Roland recognized one name, the *Leyte Gulf.*

"The Ibarran fleet strength is known," Lettow said, "and we will arrive with enough firepower to overmatch them. If they want to fight, they'll lose quickly. I'm counting on their ship captains preferring honorable surrender than a pathetic blaze of glory. Let me address the elephant in the room—why the Ibarras went rogue."

The holo changed to a large civilian ship in orbit over Luna. The ship exploded, and Roland frowned, trying to remember when such a tragedy happened.

"That's the *Hiawatha*, a civilian transport with more than three thousand men and women aboard," Lettow said. "She was lost soon after the incident with the Ruhaald and Naroosha was resolved. I have to call it an 'incident' because saying we blew those treacherous Naroosha shits out of the sky and forced the squids to surrender," he nodded to the armor soldiers in the front row, "is not said in polite company as the Ruhaald are friendly with us these days.

"The initial investigation into the loss of the *Hiawatha* yielded nothing actionable, and the matter was shelved. Navy CSI took a second look at the loss and found that Marc Ibarra was responsible for the explosion, and a sealed indictment was prepared to charge him with several thousand counts of murder and other crimes." Lettow shook his head. "He must have gotten wind of what was happening, as he and Stacey Ibarra managed to co-opt the 13th Fleet before it was set to be decommissioned and flee with it through the Crucible."

Roland leaned toward Gideon and whispered, "Sir, what about the Hale—"

Gideon silenced him with a glance.

"Further," Lettow's face darkened, "High Command is certain the Ibarras were responsible for the destruction of the *Cairo* and the disappearance of the 92nd Reconnaissance Squadron in the Vespus system. No matter the Ibarras' history, no matter what they've done for Earth, this will not stand. It ends in Oricon.

"I hereby issue Fleet Directive number two-delta. All Ibarra-flagged vessels and associated personnel that do not respond to any and all orders to surrender are to be treated as hostile. Any aggressive acts on their part are to be answered with force until such time as they are destroyed or surrender. Any questions?"

"Sir," a female commander stood up a few rows behind Roland, "the 13th had barely a skeleton crew when it…went off the books. How combat-effective are their ships with that level of manpower?"

Smart question, Roland thought. *She's beating around the bush to get the answer to a bigger issue.*

Lettow tapped a small stack of data slates together on his lectern.

"I asked the Intelligence Ministry the same question," he said. "They don't have a definite answer. Assume their ships are fully mission-capable until we learn otherwise."

Roland frowned. The spies must not know if the Ibarras had a procedural-generation facility. He was a frontline fighter, trained to break the enemy's will and body, not to divine their intentions, but that knowledge gap struck him as a significant weakness in Lettow's plan.

"Anything else? If not, religious observances are scheduled for 2030 hours. Captain Sobieski," Lettow looked down to the Uhlan lance's commander, "those that keep to the Saint meet in cargo bay twelve. Can any of you attend?"

Sobieski beat a fist to his chest.

"Resiste et mords," Lettow walked off the stage and the audience rose to their feet.

Conversations broke out around Roland. He overheard ship captains rattling off pre-battle instructions, a few officers expressing disbelief at the Ibarras' turn for the worse, staffers from the squadrons within the fleet trying to get the others' attention. He hadn't been in the Armor Corps for long, but long enough to know that most of a staff's work got done in the minutes after a meeting, never during a meeting.

Gideon glanced down at his watch, then brought his soldiers over with a small gesture with one hand.

"Suit up," he said. "We're first on deck for VR range, then live-fire qualifications."

"Sir, if we're green across the board," Roland said, "can we attend the service?"

"Mission prep is the top priority. If that's in order, then you can go." Gideon looked over Roland's shoulder.

Roland turned around and came face-to-face with Captain Sobieski, a slight man a bit shorter than Roland and with thinning hair.

"You're both supplicants," he said, glancing at the bare spots on their chest where a Templar Cross would be. "First battle service? Of course. You attend in armor. Arrive as soon as you can."

Gideon tapped Roland on the arm.

"Daylight's burning, move out," the lieutenant said.

CHAPTER 5

Admiral Lettow paced back and forth in front of his personal shuttle in the smallest bay on the *Ardennes*. That he'd been ordered to show up here—alone, no less—by President Garret was an order he had no qualms with. That he'd been here for almost ten minutes irked him to no end.

He looked out the open bay doors. As nice as the view of Luna and Earth was, his time and attention were the most valuable commodities he had, and right now he was wasting them.

"If this was some sort of joke, I will keelhaul every last…"

The force field separating the bay from the

void shimmered, and spindly, gunmetal-gray spider legs the size of tree branches crept around the edge of the doors. An object shaped like a stretched egg with several stalks stuck to it crawled into the bay, its body easily twice the size of Lettow. Fractals swirled over its surface.

Lettow knew what is was. He'd seen them in his nightmares since the Battle of Ceres.

A Xaros drone.

He backed away, reaching for a weapon on his hip that wasn't there.

The drone landed on the deck and the legs drew into the shell. It morphed into a humanoid shape, then coalesced into a tall, athletic woman with blond hair and a well-lined face.

"I won't bite," she said.

Lettow spun around and reached for the door controls, but a firm hand grabbed him by the wrist. He looked into Torni's face, then back to the open bay doors.

"Most call me Keeper," she said. "I used to be Torni."

As Lettow pulled his hand back, Torni held on for a just a moment so he could gauge her strength, then she let him go.

"By the Saint…what are you?" Lettow asked.

"Highly classified. What I'm about to share with you is even more hush-hush, which is why I had to deliver this in person," she said.

"Torni…"

"You've seen that damn movie about the Dotari, just like everyone else." She rolled her eyes. "I'll tell you that having your death reimagined on film is nothing to be proud of."

"I am…confused."

"What's not in that flick is what really happened. A Xaros Master made a copy of my…" she tapped her head then her heart, "to tear apart at his leisure. Then he murdered me. What he copied managed to escape with a bit of help and now I'm like this. The general public would not take it well that a Xaros drone controls the Crucible over Ceres and the Union's interstellar travel. Understand?"

"Understood."

"There's more to Oricon than just the Ibarras, and I am here to give you your orders—your unofficial but direct orders. This comes straight from the president," she added, raising an eyebrow at him.

Lettow nodded.

"The Qa'Resh…the public knows them as the species that founded the Alliance that saved us from the Xaros. The truth is a bit more complicated. The true Qa'Resh civilization vanished from the galaxy millions of years ago, but they left caretakers behind to guide any space-faring civilizations that would come after them."

"They were the first intelligent life?" Lettow asked.

Torni shook her head slowly.

"That's a sad story for another day," she said. "But when the Qa'Resh ascended—vanished, sorry—they left some things behind. Our Path Finder teams spent years combing through every world we thought the Qa'Resh might have touched.

To the best of our knowledge, they were the most technologically advanced species that ever lived in the Milky Way, superior even to the Xaros."

"Anything they left behind would be invaluable," Lettow said.

"'Invaluable' is an understatement. A quantum leap in technology, society…it would have more of an impact on human history than the Ember War. We've found fragments here and there—most of it indecipherable—but then someone had a breakthrough." She held up a palm and a hologram of an object that looked like a conch shell made of silver.

"The Qa'Resh left behind a ship," she said. "We found reference to it from more than one extinct species. A sort of chariot of the gods. We were close to finding it when…the woman who made the breakthrough left Earth."

"Stacey Ibarra," Lettow said.

"Correct, and we've been two steps behind her on the search for the Qa'Resh ark. That she's stuck her head up in the Oricon system must mean there's something important there for her, and she's obsessed with the ark."

"The ark is the real reason she left Earth?"

"Her why is hard to pin down—her accident at the end of the war, the end of the proccie program. I think it was a broken heart that pushed her over the edge. But what matters is that she wants the ship. And so does Earth. You are to secure Stacey Ibarra and whatever she's found on Oricon by any means necessary. Nothing else matters."

"The colonists—"

"Nothing else matters, Admiral. If the Ibarras get their hands on the ark—or any significant piece of Qa'Resh technology—it is over. The very survival of humanity depends on this."

"Then send more ships with me," he said.

"I can barely get your fleet through the Crucible to Oricon. If we could send more, I would. We're putting a lot of special trust and faith in you, Admiral." She canted her head to one side. "I must get back to the Crucible."

She turned and walked back to the open bay doors where stalks grew out of her back and lifted her off the deck.

"Wait—is there anything else I should know?" Lettow asked.

Torni turned back, the surface of her shell fading to gray, and said, "Stacey…she's not well. If you come across Marc Ibarra, he may be more reasonable. Good luck." She morphed into her drone form and flew out of the cargo bay.

****

Roland and Aignar, both in armor, ascended through the *Ardennes* in a maintenance lift. Blast doors unlocked and recessed into the walls as they went along, then banged shut as they cleared each deck. The whir of gears and clang of metal marked each new level, a harsh industrial replacement for the pleasant ding of a civilian elevator.

"You never did this when you were a crunchy?" Roland asked.

"Didn't find the Saint until after I got hit," Aignar said. He lifted an armored hand and moved his fingers in a smooth wave.

"How does the armor feel compared to your prosthetics?" Roland asked.

"I am armor. I am…whole. If I could, I'd never leave the womb, but if I didn't, then the little of what's left of the broken part of me would wither away. Did I ever tell you that I could sing? I was good. Could do the classics from Sinatra, Broden, Bublé, Draiman. But this…" He beat his fists against his chest twice, the clash of metal on metal ringing through the lift shaft. "This is better."

Roland's helm nodded. Deep down, he wasn't sure if Aignar was telling the truth to himself or to Roland.

They stopped and cargo-bay doors opened to a tall, wide room bereft of any cargo or machinery. To their left, ranks of sailors and Rangers stood in silent prayer. Opposite them were a half-dozen armor all bent to a knee. Red-armored Uhlans, all bearing the Crusader cross outlined in gold, had their helms bent to the hilt of massive swords, tips resting against the deck. Two armor soldiers from the Chasseurs lance formed a line with them, one with the cross and sword, the other with his sword-less arm resting on his bent knee.

"Fall in to my left and kneel." Sobieski sent to the two Iron Dragoons over infrared coms, keeping their conversation private from the rest of the bay. "The ceremony will begin soon."

Roland noted open bay doors behind the armor and across the bay behind the sailors and others. The un-armored only entered through the door opposite the Templar. Roland did as instructed, keeping his left forearm across his knee, right fist to the deck.

"Speak the prayer with the chaplain," Sobieski said. "They taught you the rest on Mars?"

"Yes, sir," Aignar said.

"Good...chaplain's on his way." Sobieski closed the channel.

Roland angled one of the cameras in his helm up to look at the throng of the faithful. The crowd filled the back half of the bay and had bunched up through the bay doors.

"I didn't know so many even knew of the Saint," Roland said to Aignar on a private channel.

"There's a shrine on every ship now," Aignar said. "They're here to ask for protection, for her to witness them in the fight so they may be judged worthy if they die. That armor is here makes a difference. Only armor is ever allowed into her tomb. To them, we are Saint Kallen made manifest, her sword and her shield."

"How do you know all this?"

"While Tongea was teaching you the way of the sword, I studied the catechism."

The ship's chaplain walked out from between the armor, a censer and chain in his hands. He held the gunmetal censer aloft and red incense billowed out.

Roland raised his fist and slammed it against the deck, in time with the rap of sword points and fists from the other armor. He waited for a five count, then hit the deck two more times.

The chaplain let the censer run out through his hands, stopping it a few inches above his foot. He swung it from side to side and walked across the front rank of the faithful, most of them Rangers in full battle armor, their visors painted with skulls.

Roland increased the sensitivity on his armor's olfactory sensors and smelled the iron tang of Mars carried on the incense.

"May the Saint protect us," the chaplain said loudly. Roland activated his armor's speakers.

"*Sancti spiritus adsit nobis gratia,*" the armor intoned.

"May the Saint witness us." The chaplain said, continuing his march up the front row.

"*Kallen, ferrum corde,*" the armor continued the prayer.

"May we find the iron in our hearts to prove worthy of her."

"*Perducat nos ad portam salutis. Amen.*"

The forward line of Rangers rose to their feet and crossed the bay. The chaplain turned around and walked to the other end of the bay, the censer still swinging, still sending red smoke into the air.

The Templars began chanting the pre-battle hymn in Latin.

A Ranger walked to Roland, lifted his visor, and beat a fist against his heart, then rapped twice against Roland's leg. He slammed his visor down and continued through the doors behind the armor. The next Ranger did the same thing, as did the procession of sailors coming from behind them.

"What're they doing?" Roland asked Aignar over their IR.

"We are armor. We are the Saint. One last prayer from them before battle," Aignar said.

Roland turned his helm slightly, watching as the crew passed by the armor.

"It's like…Memorial Square," Roland said. "You've been there? The armor that died at the last battle with the Xaros, all in a circle around the platform. You could walk between the statues up to a platform inside. Look out over their shoulders and…I always felt protected when I was there.

We're recreating that moment, aren't we?"

"That's right. I thought you skipped all the catechism lessons?"

Roland took in the faces of those passing by, tapping against his armor. The throng through the back of the bay hadn't stopped.

"I'm staying here…" Roland said, "until the last moment before the battle if needed."

"For them," a voice said.

"What?" Roland asked.

"I didn't say anything." Aignar turned his helm to his lance mate.

Roland lifted his fist off the deck and opened his hand, feeling the touch of the men and women as they passed by.

CHAPTER 6

Lettow blinked away the jump gate's afterglow and slapped his palm against the buckle on his chest. Straps unlocked and zipped back into his seat as he sprang up and went to his round holo tank the size of a dinner table for twelve.

His staff arrived at their positions within seconds, all of them too slow to beat the admiral to battle stations.

"Ops, what's our situation?" Lettow asked.

"Data's coming in garbled," a captain said from the admiral's right. "Keeper warned this might happen—quantum fluctuations in the wormholes playing hell with our systems."

The *Ardennes* appeared in the center of the tank, then the massive Crucible gate they'd arrived through. Icons for the 14th Fleet's ships came up, some bouncing from spot to spot as corrupted telemetry data came in.

"We are out of formation." Lettow spread out his hands on the tank edge and prayed that the Ibarras weren't waiting just beyond effective sensor range to spring an ambush and crush his scattered ships one by one.

"We've eyes on Oricon," the ops captain said. The moon appeared in the tank, orbiting the tan gas giant, Oricon Prime. "Telescopes pulling images now…Auburn City's on the other side of the moon, but we've got eyes on one settlement."

"Show me," Lettow said.

Grainy images came through of a town nestled in a mountain valley where hyperloop tubes converged into a dome at the town center. Smoke rose from several buildings. Lettow zoomed in along the edge of the settlement and saw hasty barricades ringing the town. He zoomed in on two shadows, both of which looked human.

"Have we been able to raise them?" Lettow asked.

"All we're getting from the moon is static," his XO said from his left. "There's some sort of ionization in the atmosphere blocking our hails. Not something that's ever happened to Oricon, according to the colony logs."

"Stranger and stranger…" Lettow clasped his hands behind his back. "Launch recon probes. Any sign of—"

Threat icons appeared next to another of Oricon Prime's moons, Satsunan, far from the colony world.

"Got an EM hit off a *Gibraltar*-class battlecruiser," his Operations captain said. "Fleet sensor's going to work now. Looks like the *Matterhorn*, one of the 13th."

Lettow reached out and touched the moon to bring it to the center of the tank, crowding out the rest of the system.

The white-and-red-colored hull of a

battlecruiser orbited Satsunan. More ships materialized as the sensors collected more and more data. The battlecruiser's hull was blackened in parts, bleeding atmosphere from rents in her armor. Her rail cannon batteries fired and Lettow glanced to one side to check the range between his fleet and the *Matterhorn*. More and more Ibarran ships came around the moon.

"What're they shooting at?" the admiral asked. "No main gun's going to have a chance of scoring a hit on us from that distance."

"Think I've got it," the XO said. He traced a line along the rail cannon munition's path and frowned when a brief fireball erupted in the middle of empty space. "That's funny."

"'Funny,'" Lettow deadpanned.

"I mean sensor suites are being re-tasked and…" The tank changed view. In the void between moons, a fleet made up of dozens of angular ships appeared. The onyx and dusky red hulls melded against the backdrop of space, occasionally occulting the stars beyond. Smaller ships resembled a grasping hand with six fingers, all somewhat irregular and none identical to the others. Larger vessels bore outcroppings, like burnt willow branches.

"Almost nothing from the fleet on a full-spectrum sweep," the XO said. "We can barely read them on radar." Blue-white bolts of energy snapped from the ships and sped toward the Ibarrans.

"Who are they?" Lettow asked. "They're not Vishrakath."

"Ships match nothing in the target database," the ops captain said.

"Ibarra fleet changing course," the XO said. A dashed line traced away from the rebel ships and wrapped around the gas giant.

"Same with the unidentified ships," the ops captain said. "They're maneuvering out of weapons range."

"Now they know we're here." Lettow drummed his fingers against the holo tank. "Seems to me that neither of them knows what side we're on. If either one thought we were with them, they'd press the attack. They broke off the fight because we might help the other side and they need to run. Hail them, standard first-contact protocol for both fleets. Let's see how they answer."

"Aye aye," the XO said.

Lettow traced a circle on a screen and a contact node came up. He jammed a fingertip onto Captain Sobieski's name.

****

Roland felt the power leads from his suit connect to an external battery and a new display came up on his HUD. Technicians scrambled up and down his supine armor fit into a torpedo housing, like he was Gulliver in the land of Lilliput.

"Sir, you okay in there?" Henrique tapped a wrench against Roland's breastplate.

"I am armor," Roland said, "inside a torpedo. Soon to be inside a torpedo tube. It will get more interesting after that."

"*Fique tranquilo,* sir," the Brazilian said,

"but better you than me, right?"

"And I thought dropping through a hellhole on the *Scipio* was a novel way to make planetfall," Aignar said over the lance frequency. He was two torpedoes away, his tech team working just as frantically as Roland's to get him installed.

"I can understand the genesis of the concept," Cha'ril said from her tube. "One can assume armor won't get claustrophobic and can withstand the acceleration."

"Do you think it was someone in the Armor Corps that woke up one morning and said, 'Why don't we just *shoot* our armor at things,' or was it some navy engineer that got a visit from the good-idea fairy and wanted to impress her boss with a crazy idea that would work on paper?" Aignar asked.

"I think Gideon tested the prototypes," Cha'ril said. "Maybe that's why we got tasked with this mission. Once he's off the line with Sobieski, you can ask him."

Roland looked at the lance leader's icon in

his HUD. It was ringed with a pulsating blue line indicating a private conversation.

"So it's definitely the Ibarra fleet," Roland said, "and some unknown species. Nice and complicated, just like I like my wars."

"You think the Ibarras—the actual Ibarras—are in system?" Aignar asked.

"Tough one. When was the last time anyone even saw them? They dropped off the face of the Earth after the Ember War ended," Roland said.

"My father saw Stacey Ibarra on Dotari," Cha'ril said. She transmitted a slideshow to Roland and Aignar of an elderly Dotari lying in an upright glass coffin. Dotari in white togas took up the right half of the images; humans and several other species were on the left.

"Ambassador Pa'lon's funeral," she said. "Quite the event. Surviving members of the old embassies on Bastion came to pay their respects. Having so many species together undoubtedly led to the decision to jointly develop New Bastion and—"

"Did he see her or not?" Aignar asked.

The images skipped forward and stopped on a human woman in a black dress, her hands covered by gloves, her face obscured with a heavy veil.

"That's her," Cha'ril said. "She didn't speak at the funeral, which I'm told is a human custom. Given her relationship with Pa'lon and her history with the Dotari, it was something of a surprise that she remained silent through the ceremony. My father mentioned that she must have been miserable in that gown, as it was unseasonably chilly that day."

"I just pinged the ship's data banks," Aignar said. "Not a single article or interview with her since the end of the war. I thought High Command might have scrubbed her from the records, given the mess, but do any of you remember her in the news?"

"Nope," Roland said. "She was on the vids all the time during the war…I had a bit of a crush on her back then."

"Me too. I always liked the demure types," Aignar said. "Then I married and divorced a redneck type. Serves me right."

"I never developed a prepubescent affinity for her," Cha'ril said. "But what of Marc Ibarra? All recordings of him after the Earth was liberated from the Xaros are of a hologram."

"Rumor mill says he died during the first invasion," Roland said, "then that Qa'Resh probe he'd been working with stored his soul—or something like that—inside itself and kept him 'alive.' That's why we always saw him as a hologram."

"But he was on the *Breitenfeld* for the final assault on the Xaros Dyson sphere," Aignar said. "Him in person. Plenty of crew saw him there."

"Humans have the technology to transfer their minds from computers to new bodies?" Cha'ril asked.

"Maybe the Qa'Resh could do it," Aignar said. "You'd think if that sort of quasi-immortality was available, people would be lining up for the chance. That must be what happened—the probe put Marc Ibarra into a proccie body—and then the most infamous man in human history decided to fade into obscurity."

"Do you two hold any animosity toward him? Before the *Cairo*?" Cha'ril asked.

"He was in a tough spot," Roland said. "What he did with the fleet that survived the first wave of Xaros…I don't know if there was a perfect solution. Imagine you're one of five children in a burning house. A fireman breaks down the door and has just enough time to save one kid. If you're that kid, do you hate the fireman for not saving the others?"

"Jesus, little brutal with the metaphor, kid," Aignar said.

"Marc Ibarra let 99.9-something percent of the human species die," Roland said. "No warning. No chance to flee. He had his fleet sidestep the invasion, then return just in time—when the Xaros were weak and the Crucible was nearly complete. All part of his plan. Then—"

"Then we won the war and survived extinction," Cha'ril said.

"It's hard to judge," Roland said. "In the grand scheme of things, I'm sure the consensus will go back and forth between hating him and praising him. It's not up to us to judge him, just to bring him to justice for the *Hiawatha,* the *Cairo,* and all the other lives lost that he's responsible for since the end of the war."

"Dragoons." Gideon returned to the lance channel. "We have our target. Small town at a hyperloop nexus called Tonopah. No contact with the residents, but the ship can see them moving around the town's defenses."

"Why not the main settlement, Auburn?" Roland asked.

"We can't see it. Moon's facing the wrong way," Gideon said. "The admiral doesn't want to risk sending anyone over there blind. That all the recon probes vanished soon as they crossed over the horizon leads me to agree with him. The fleet needs answers, and we can get them from Tonopah. We'll be within Terrestrial Insertion Torpedo range in ten minutes."

"That acronym—"

"Is not final," Gideon cut Aignar off. "I told the engineers the name lacks...nuance. What is important is at what altitude you eject. Too soon and you'll burn up on reentry. Too late and you're a smear against a mountain and the designers assume there's a design flaw. So listen carefully."

CHAPTER 7

The amniosis fluid surrounding Roland sloshed against his body. The inner wall of the womb pressed in tighter, almost squeezing him.

He remained focused on the course projection on his HUD and watched the distance counter tick closer and closer to zero.

"—nd by," Gideon said. The channel opened up and broadcast a squeal.

Their landing torpedoes just entered Oricon's upper atmosphere and the heat bloom would render any and all IR communication impossible.

BREAKING. BREAKING. Flashed across

his HUD.

A shudder passed through his womb as rocket nozzles rose along the length of the torpedo and fired. The sudden deceleration bumped the top of his head against his womb hard enough to send a bolt of pain down his back. The inner wall of his womb gripped tighter, almost swaddling him.

Found a design flaw, he thought. *Maybe I'll write a strongly worded letter to the engineers…assuming I manage to land with more grace than a raw egg thrown at a wall.*

The rumble of deceleration ended and data returned to his HUD. The torpedo's path arced just over a snowcapped mountain ridge, one approaching far faster than Roland felt comfortable with. The lower ring of his projected path clipped the jagged peaks.

He dialed up the emergency release and stopped. If he ejected now, he would hit the snow-covered slope and likely trigger an avalanche. If he waited, he ran the risk of plowing into the mountain at full—and fatal—speed.

Please don't be designed by the lowest bidder. Please don't be—

The torpedo cleared the mountain top with a few feet to spare, kicking up a vortex of snow and rock as he passed.

Very angry letter. So angry.

His HUD pulsed yellow and forward panels on the torpedo lifted up. The metal sides peeled away and fluttered through the air like petals caught in a gale and Roland could finally see with his armor's own sensors. He pressed his arms out and threw off the last of the vehicle's frame.

A quick scan highlighted a small arc of the hyperloop between ridgelines. No power sources. No composite metals. No transmissions.

The landscape's trees looked like black moss as he fell to the surface. He cycled power into his jetpack and waited to pass into the landing buffer, which his HUD displayed as a red augmented-reality box fifty meters off the ground.

Roland waited until he'd nearly passed through the bottom of the box before activating his jetpack. The jerk from the rocket's firing was almost a playground tag compared to the insertion torpedo's breaking maneuver. He ejected the jetpack a few yards over the ground and slid to a stop through a dry stream bed.

His shoulder-mounted rotary gun sprang up and began spinning. He raised his arm with the twin gauss cannons and scanned around further…nothing.

Three heat blossoms appeared overhead and the rest of his lance came down just ahead of him. Roland took off running, his massive legs pounding against bare rocks and echoing through the valley. There was no mistaking the Iron Dragoons' arrival; the time for subtlety was past.

Gideon landed at a run, making his entire descent look almost second nature to him.

Aignar would have tripped over a boulder had his armor not shattered it with a kick. Roland ran alongside his lance mate and kept his pace.

"Roland, did you intentionally alter your course to clip the mountain?" Cha'ril asked.

"The guidance computer didn't compensate for snowpack," Roland said. "And I almost got a concussion during the breaking maneuver. I can tell the designers didn't participate in hands-on testing. Not sure how Mars can make that happen."

Gideon had pulled ahead of Roland and Aignar. Cha'ril fell back, forming them into a diamond formation with the lieutenant leading the way.

"Same as having riggers jump the parachutes they packed themselves," Gideon said. "Older reference, but the idea was put before the design committee."

"I can imagine the engineers' response," Aignar said. "'But did you die? No? Full production!'"

"Can it." Gideon said, sending a travel route to the lance, a rally point at the base of a spur on the mountainside opposite Tonopah Valley. "We'll do a quick recon from there."

Roland acknowledged the route and kept scanning their right flank. The Oricon trees were tall and spindly, with dark bark and wide, thorny canopies. Running past the surrounding forests and the snow-covered mountainsides was like looking at a bar code from some antique price sticker.

Gideon slowed as he approached a drop-off next to the rally point. He skidded to a halt and aimed his weapons down the slope to an area Roland couldn't see.

"Contact?" Aignar asked.

"I'm not sure what this is," the lieutenant said. "Roland, down here with me. Rest of you on security."

Roland jogged over, his feet crushing the smooth rocks of a dry stream bed into powder. Gideon stood at the edge of a spread of what looked like large red eggshells, all cracked apart and nestled into a bed of lime-green ooze.

"Some sort of local…plant?" Roland asked.

Gideon picked up a piece of the red eggshell. Goo ran through his fingers and dripped slowly to the ground. He squeezed, deforming it with a squeal of tortured metal.

"Tensile strength is high. My sensors can't get a composition read on it, but the sludge is organic," Gideon said.

Roland spied another piece jutting out of the green substance. A discoloration just beneath the surface caught the setting sun's light. He activated his olfactory sensors and cringed inside his armor. The scent brought him back to one of his first days working as a busboy, when he'd been ordered to clean up soft-drink syrup that had leaked in a storeroom. The stench of rotting syrup permeated that room and never seemed to go away, no matter how many times he cleaned it.

He picked up the metal…and twisted it around to show Gideon a pair of bullet holes.

"15-millimeter," Roland said. "My sensors show a tungsten and cobalt residue on the inside of the holes. This was done with gauss weapons."

"Our cannons are 30-millimeter. Ammo for gauss rifles and carbines is half the size of what we're looking at," Gideon said. "Whoever did this wasn't using Terran standard equipment."

"It was a massacre." Roland tossed the metal back into the field. He activated the pilot light for his flamethrower and burned green residue off his armor's fingers. "These must be soldiers from that unidentified alien fleet."

"Fair assessment, but don't cling to it," Gideon said. "Get eyes on the settlement."

"Sir." Roland walked up the spur and ran a sensor arm up from his helm. Smoke rose from a few buildings in Tonopah. The tops of prefab buildings stuck out over the hasty barricades of hyperloop parts and wrecked vehicles. Incomplete rail lines mounted atop columns dotted the surrounding valley, all pointing to a nexus point in the middle of the town.

"Don't see much activity," Roland said. "No transmissions eith—"

The slope next to Roland exploded in a rain of loose dirt and rock fragments, and Roland slid back down, his armor covered in dust.

"That was a rail rifle," Cha'ril said.

"I noticed." Roland tapped the side of his

helm twice to knock dirt from his optics.

"They seem a bit twitchy," Aignar said.

"We're in an enemy position," Gideon said. "They must not know what happened out here—or that help's arrived."

"Some welcome," Roland said.

"If we wish to avoid another rail shot," Cha'ril motioned to a nearby stand of trees, "perhaps we should signal our intentions."

Aignar planted a foot against a tree trunk and snapped it apart with a quick tug. He broke another and held the two trees like batons.

"My semaphore is weak," he said. "Anyone remember how to send 'Don't shoot me'?"

"Wave the tree tops over the slope," Gideon said. "They should get the message."

****

On a holo map of Oricon, a dashed circle pulsed over Auburn.

"Scopes saw the armor disembark from their

insertion torps," Strickland said. "That high G of a maneuver didn't look pleasant, but if anyone can shrug off that level of abuse, it's the armor."

"But no contact from that first lance?" Lettow asked.

"Negative. I'd say it's from whatever's scrambling commo in the atmosphere, not any issue with the landing," Strickland said.

"Launch the rest of the armor to Auburn City," Lettow swiped the picture aside and brought up a high altitude image from a probe. All their initial surveillance drones had failed to report back after entering the atmosphere. The next batch swung around the moon and sent back decent images. The colony's main city looked largely intact, with some damaged buildings still smoking. The drones had picked up several work crews moving around the city. The colonists were still there, but they weren't able to talk to his fleet.

"Aye aye," Strickland said.

Lettow zoomed the holo tank out and looked over the system. His fleet hadn't progressed far from the Crucible gate. The Ibarra ships and the unknown aliens were still moving apart, though the aliens seemed to be in less of a hurry than the other humans.

Amber light lit up around the inner wall of the holo tank. The holo shifted to the Crucible, where tiny flashes of light sparkled between the great black thorns making up the gate.

"What the hell?" Lettow magnified the gate and saw cracks running along the thorns.

"Explosives," Strickland said. "Are they trying to destroy it? That's insane. We could be trapped here forever."

The flashes died away and Lettow felt a ball of ice in his stomach. He opened a channel to his captains.

"All ships, come about and return to the Crucible," Lettow said. He watched as cracks grew through the thorns…then slowed to a halt. The gaps began closing of their own accord, but far slower than the speed at which the damage was done.

"The control nodes are wrecked," Strickland

said. "We couldn't go back through if we tried. The Xaros built them to self-repair, but I don't know how long that will take."

"And no one's getting in or out until that happens." Lettow shook his head. The game had just changed.

He opened a channel to Commander Rusk, his chief engineer.

"Commander, get survey teams onto the Crucible as soon as possible. I need an estimate on when it'll be operational again," he said.

"And Oricon? The enemy?" Strickland asked.

"We lose the Crucible and we'll have worse problems than whatever they're up to," the admiral said. "I need to know more by the time we have the gate up and running. Either the armor will get it to us or someone will decide to start talking."

****

The Iron Dragoons waited outside the

barricades as a truck pulled a gate open. A length of metal pitted with scorch marks and bullet strikes fell free and clattered against the ground, and a man and a woman in heavy jackets and holding standard-issue gauss rifles stood in the middle of the road just within the hasty barricades.

Villagers crowded around side streets, struggling to catch a glimpse of the armored warriors.

Gideon led his lance inside. He knelt to one knee in front of the pair, bringing his helm almost eye level with them.

"Did you find them?" asked a heavyset man with a thick beard. "The others said you were out there looking, but we haven't heard anything for hours."

"This day just gets weirder and weirder," Aignar said on the lance's private IR channel.

"I am First Lieutenant Gideon, Iron Dragoons, 2nd Regiment of the Terran Armored Corps," Gideon said. "We made Crucible gate transit nine hours ago and planetfall not long ago. I do not know who, or what, you're talking about."

"Earth is here," the woman said. "About God damn time. If it wasn't for the Legion, the Kesaht would have taken *all* of us, not just the children."

"I need you to start at the beginning," Gideon said.

"I'm Tim Dinkins, project head and foreman out here," the bearded man said. "This is my wife, Sally. Auburn City put out a general alert a few days ago when the Kesaht fleet arrived. They started landing troops and all our commo with the city went down. Then we lost contact with work crews and the primary-school field trip out at Lorraine Falls. The Legion is out there looking for them…they. They didn't say anything to you? Our two boys are still out there. Forty-seven children in all. They didn't say anything to you?"

"What happened after you lost contact?" Gideon asked.

"The Legion showed up. I thought they were doughboys the first time I saw them, but they're just that damn big," Dinkins said. "They helped us get organized and fought off the Kesaht for days. Then they all left a few hours ago, said reinforcements were on the way and they'd find our missing children and work crews."

"How is this news to you?" Sally asked. "I did my stint in uniform. I know how crazy things get in a fight, but I don't understand how armor—*armor*—can drop into a war zone blind."

"A moment…" Gideon stood up and switched to the lance's IR channel.

"They don't know the Ibarras went renegade," Roland said.

"Isn't exactly common knowledge," Aignar said. "Doubt these Legion-types showed up and gave them a primer on their politics."

"If they're renegades, why would they fight to protect these other humans?" Cha'ril asked. "I am a novice at human history, but your internecine splits are rarely peaceful."

"The Kesaht and Ibarrans show up at the same place and at the same time," Gideon said.

"Not a coincidence."

"What about the missing children?" Roland asked.

"That's our best chance of figuring this out," Gideon said. "If we find the lost, they'll be with the Ibarrans or these Kesaht. Either way, we'll get answers."

"Bet they can tell us more about this Legion," Aignar said. "Probably best to keep that we're here to rein in the Ibarras close to the chest. Let's not guess which side this outpost would take if they had to choose."

"Fair enough." Gideon went back to the Dinkinses.

A young man with a rail sniper rifle strapped to his back pushed his way through the crowd. He went pale and tried to elbow his way back when he saw Roland's helm fixated on him.

"You," Roland boomed from his speakers as he pointed at the sniper.

The sniper froze and the crowd backed away from him.

"I'm sorry!" the sniper squeaked and he lowered his head like a dog about to be struck. "Your optic popped up at the last place we saw the Rakka massing and I thought…that…"

"Do your sights have combat footage?" Roland asked.

"My what?" The sniper looked up sheepishly.

"Vortex mark 9 sights. They keep a recording of thirty seconds before and after every shot for evaluation." Roland bent down and brought his helm close to the sniper.

"I admit it was me, okay? Just don't crush my skull. I missed!"

"I want to see the enemy." Roland reached for the rifle on the man's back.

"Don't touch that!" the sniper shouted. "Don't you ever touch my Fanny without asking!"

The crowd, which had been watching intently before, fell silent.

"You named your rifle…Fanny?" Roland asked.

The sniper's head bobbed up and down. "I did. Yes. It seemed like a great idea up until this exact instant."

Data wires popped out of the base of Roland's wrist.

"Connect me to your optics," Roland said. The sniper slung the bolt half off his back and plugged the wires into the boxy sites.

"What's your name?" Roland asked.

"John Johansson. But everyone calls me Jo. And I'm really sorry I almost shot you."

"I'm Roland. There's a fog in war. One we do our best to see through. I'm just glad that you missed. Shoot straighter next time you see a …Rakka or a Kesaht."

"The grunts are the Rakka. The whole bunch of alien shitheads are the Kesaht," Jo said.

Roland's computers downloaded the last of the sniper's footage and shared it with the rest of his lance. He drew the wires back into his armor and stood up.

"If there's someone else with footage from

the battle, please bring it over," Roland said.

Jo gave him a thumbs-up and ran back into the city.

Roland watched the most recent video and was surprised that the sniper managed to spot the optic as it peeked around rocks along the ridgeline. He went to the next file.

The clip began with the rifle pointed down at the inner wall of the barricade. The snap of gauss weapons and a hissing slash of energy weapons sounded through the background.

"Controller in this sector!" a deep voice boomed. "Take it out, Jo!"

The rifle swung up and across a soldier in black armor. Roland paused the feed and went back frame by frame until he found a decent image of the soldier. The power armor looked little different from the combat suits worn by the Rangers—thick armor plates over a pseudo-muscle layer that boosted the wearer's strength and made wearing the heavy armor possible. The soldier carried an oversized gauss rifle, not of any design Roland had ever seen before. His face was hidden beneath a matte-black visor; the only marking on his armor was of an eagle within a laurel on his left shoulder.

So this is a legionnaire, he thought.

Roland's computers measured the legionnaire from the camera angle and gave the man's height at over six and a half feet tall. Unarmored weight at two hundred twenty pounds—by his build, none of it fat.

"They've got some big boys," Aignar said. He sent an image capture from another video. Eight of the legionnaires, all similarly large and imposing, firing through the barricade. Roland magnified a section in the background. A legionnaire lay dead in a pool of blood, chest armor mangled.

"Sir." Roland said and sent the picture to Gideon.

"Did they leave any wounded behind?" Gideon asked the foreman.

"No," Dinkins said. "Any that were hurt managed to walk out of here. They flash-burned their dead and took the ashes with them. Not sure when the army started doing that."

"Look at this." Cha'ril sent a picture to the lance: a mob of red-armored aliens with wide, hunched shoulders charging toward the town, all wielding rifles connected to their arms and torsos with glowing cables.

"Those must be the Rakka," Aignar said. "Armor looks like the mess we found earlier. They don't look like they're invertebrate goo creatures…some sort of biological reaction on death?"

"Not a trait we've seen in any sentient species," Cha'ril said. "A failsafe? Xaros drones disintegrated upon destruction. Kept anyone from ever reverse-engineering their technology."

"Then there's this." Aignar sent another screen capture: a taller, straight-backed figure behind the charging Rakka, partially obscured by tree trunks.

"Doesn't look like the same species," Roland said. "Maybe an evolved leadership caste? The Toth overlords were vastly different from their warriors and menials."

"Being a brain in a jar makes you vastly different than most anything," Aignar said.

"Could these be separate xeno-types working in concert?" Cha'ril asked. "That would be unusual. Only humans have ever integrated other species into their military units with my people and the Karigole."

"Interesting observations aside," Roland said, "why is there no record of them? They're using the Crucible jump gates. Every race that can do that was part of the old Alliance. We had to co-opt Xaros technology to use the network and build new gates. These Kesaht just show up out of thin air? Something doesn't add up."

"They either possess Xaros-level technology," Cha'ril said, "or someone in the old Alliance gave them the technology."

"I don't see a sky dark with killer drones, so let's assume the former," Aignar said.

"Listen up," Gideon said, breaking away from the foreman, "the locals said the Ibarras destroyed any Kesaht transports they found in the air during the initial fight. Given the terrain and that they haven't seen anything else go for orbit, there are two likely places we can find the missing colonists."

Two shaded circles appeared on Roland's map overlay, both in opposite directions from the work camp.

"If we find the missing, we'll likely find the Ibarras and the Kesaht," Gideon said.

"What's the priority?" Roland asked.

Gideon was silent for a few moments, an uncharacteristic hesitation from the lieutenant.

"The civilians," he said. "The Ibarrans fought and died to protect them. I won't let a pack of traitors do our job for us. Secure the prisoners and bring them home. Detaining the Ibarrans is secondary. You're authorized to use lethal force if they resist."

"And the Kesaht?" Cha'ril asked.

"Unless it interferes with our other missions, kill them on sight." Gideon racked gauss shells into his forearm-mounted cannons. "The camp will send up an IR relay balloon. I want hourly updates through pigeons if you're out of IR line of sight, contact reports as soon as you can send them. Roland, Cha'ril, search the eastern area. Aignar and I will go west. Good hunting."

****

Admiral Lettow reached into his holo tank and slowly turned the image of the damaged Crucible gate around. The cracks in the great construct's thorns were still visible. Work crews in vac suits flit around the damage like flies on the wounds of a felled animal.

"Commander Rusk, status report," Lettow sent to the chief engineer on the Crucible.

"Omnium stores around the gate are intact." A woman in a vac helmet came up in the holo tank. "We're feeding that into the damaged thorns, kind of like calking over a leak. Should accelerate the self-repair sequence by several days. But we're finding secondary devices all over the place. Explosives ordnance disposal teams are defusing them as soon as we find them."

"And the nature of these devices? Human or alien?" Lettow asked.

"Both, sir, which is the damnedest thing. Some are textbook sabotage devices out of Strike Marine training. Easy to deal with. Alien ones are limpet-type devices, cling right onto the spikes. They've some anti-tamper systems, but the engineers found a bypass easy enough. Not the most complex devices we've ever seen."

A picture of a crab-like device at the end of a spike tip popped up.

"Any danger of a remote detonation?" Lettow asked.

"We've got scramblers up. EOD isn't worried, but if they start running, I'm going with them."

"I want that gate repaired and safe to use as soon as possible," Lettow said.

"Should have the surface and interior swept

in another few hours," Rusk said. "The control nodes were badly damaged. Not a lot we can do about those but wait."

"I want regular updates. Lettow out."

"Why would the Ibarras and these new aliens both rig the Crucible?" Commander Strickland, Lettow's operations officer, asked.

"Keeps reinforcements out," Lettow said. "We came through and tossed a monkey wrench into their plans. I'd bet the aliens thought we were their backup, same as the Ibarras. Now we're all stuck here together."

"And whoever damaged the Crucible cut off our cavalry," Strickland said.

"I'd wager some very frustrated ship drivers on the other end of different Crucibles are trying to get in here," Lettow said.

"Admiral," the ensign at the communications station stood up and waved, "we're being hailed by the *Matterhorn,* the Ibarran ship. Audio only."

"About time," Lettow said. "Put it through."

He swiped the Crucible to the side and pulled up the system map. The Ibarra fleet was still orbiting Satsunan, well out of firing distance from the alien fleet. The aliens were on a slow vector passed Oricon and toward the Crucible. At their current velocity, Lettow and the 14th wouldn't have to deal with them for days.

A blank silhouette of a person's head and shoulders appeared in the holo tank.

"Hello?" a woman's voice asked. "Who's there?"

"This is Admiral Lettow of the Terran Union Navy. Identify yourself."

"I am Admiral Faben."

Lettow's brow furrowed. He wagged a finger at Strickland, who began tapping furiously on his control screens.

"Faben…" Lettow said. "I've been in the navy for several decades. I don't recall ever hearing about an Admiral Faben."

"Well, I've never heard of you either. So we're even," Faben snapped back.

Strickland tossed a screen capture into the holo tank. A list of every admiral in the old Atlantic Union and the new Terran Union appeared. There was no Faben on the roster. Lettow signaled to him to keep searching.

"I think we're done with pleasantries," Lettow said. "Faben, your fleet is on open mutiny. You have attacked naval ships and murdered their crews. You've engaged in unauthorized hostilities with an alien power. You will surrender immediately and prepare to receive my security teams to take command of your ships. There is no need for violence, but any disobedience will be met with appropriate force."

"I—and my fleet—are quite happy with our current situation," she said. "You stay in your yard, I'll stay in mine, and we'll both be just fine."

"Is that why you damaged the Crucible as soon as we came through?" the admiral asked. "Keep all our yards separated?"

"What?" Faben said in a sing song voice. "I would never do that. Must've been our rude house guests."

"Do not toy with me. This is the last time I'll say this," Lettow gripped the edge of his holo tank. "You will surrender—"

"I don't answer to you!" Faben shouted.

Lettow's head rocked back slightly in surprise. This Faben did not speak or act like any admiral he'd ever met.

"We stand apart from the Union. Now and forever more. Just because we used to be on the same team doesn't mean we gave up the right to self-defense. You want to put your money where your mouth is and you'll learn the same lesson we taught the other ships you sent after us. Leave. Us. Alone."

Lettow ran course projections through his holo tank. If he raised anchor and made for the Ibarran fleet, he'd leave Oricon wide open for the alien fleet. If he moved to protect the planet, the Ibarrans would have a straight shot at the Crucible gate and escape.

"Are you really so bloodthirsty that you

don't care about the colonists?" Faben asked. "The Atlantic Union Navy I served in put the lives of civilians above all else."

Anger flared in Lettow's heart. He knew Faben was trying to goad him, but he also knew she was right.

"What happened to the colony?" Lettow asked. "Why can't we reach them?"

"The Kesaht arrived with far less caution and manners than you did," Faben said. "They hit the atmosphere with one of their ionization scramblers and landed troops soon as they arrived. My fleet managed to pull them away before they could bomb the capital into slag."

"You called them the Kesaht. You've dealt with them before? Do you know some way to contact the colony?" Lettow asked.

"You threaten me and my fleet if we don't bare our throats at your command and now you want to be best friends? Don't insult me. We saved the colony. You're welcome. Good luck finishing the job."

The transmission cut out.

Lettow grumbled and punched the side of his holo tank.

"The personnel database has one record for a Faben," Strickland said. "Most of the file's been redacted. All that's available is an Ensign Faben on a manifest from the *Breitenfeld*. No first name or picture. Everything was redacted, date on that was just after the Battle of Ceres."

"Right at the start of the Ember War," Lettow said. "Her identity isn't as important as gaining control of this situation."

"What are your orders, sir?"

"We need the Crucible operational and cleared of any explosives. Then we'll have some room to maneuver. Faben said her fleet arrived before the Kesaht, but she didn't mention why she was here in the first place, and she doesn't seem to be in any hurry to leave," Lettow said. "Whatever she's after…she hasn't found it yet."

"What good does that do us?" Strickland asked.

"Know your enemy. Know yourself. Hard to secure victory if either of those is in the wind. We need to talk to Oricon, see what they can tell us."

CHAPTER 8

Roland churned along an access road, his legs transformed into treads. The armor's travel form could cover ground faster than the legged combat configuration and saved battery life in the process. The vibration in his womb was almost soothing, but the rumble from even his sound-dampened treads kept him on edge.

"Still nothing on sector scan," Cha'ril said from just behind him.

They rolled along an access road of hardened photovalic cells running parallel to a raised hyperloop line. The double tubes were incomplete, with stacks of paneling piled high every few hundred yards, waiting for robots to come and complete the job.

"Got nothing but static on radio," he said. "If the Ibarras are still out here, they're not using any Terran standard comms."

"Roland, should we be fighting the Ibarras?" she asked.

"Not like you to question orders."

"'Friends do as friends will'…an old Dotari saying. The Ibarras defended the camp and are searching for missing children. These are not the actions of an enemy," she said.

"I wish it was as cut and dried as it is with the Kesaht or Vishrakath. See them? Shoot them. Simple. The Ibarras…you want to know what scares me about them? The ones that were back at the camp were called legionnaires. That's an old human rank for the Roman Empire—'empire' being the important word. The Ibarras might not see themselves as another part of the Terran Union, but as something new and different."

"You would rather all of humanity be under

one rule?"

"It sure beats the alternative of potential enemies. Humanity is good at killing each other. We've been at it since Cain decided he didn't like living in his brother Abel's shadow. We go to the VR range and we train to shoot Vishrakath, Haesh, Naroosha…not other men and women. You've seen that tacky *Last Stand at Takeni* movie, right? Dotari were fighting those banshee things—how'd you feel about that?"

"The banshees were no longer Dotari," she said. "That they were unwillingly transformed into the Xaros' foot soldiers would not stay my hand. They would have killed my mother and I had not one of the *Breitenfeld*'s Strike Marines saved us…which reminds me. I need to go back to Bailey's bar once we're on leave."

"Why aren't you going back to Dotari?"

"Stop distracting me," she snapped. "Focus on your assigned sector before your small talk gets us killed."

"Yes, ma'am." Roland switched to IR

sensors and swept the area ahead of them. A blur of cool air cut through the edge of the forest that made up the bulk of their search area. "Got a temperature inversion. Might be a ravine we can use to get closer without being detected."

"Then switch to combat config and lead on," she said.

Roland leaned forward and widened the distance between his treads. He planted both hands against the road and rolled forward, snapping his treads back into their leg housings as they lifted off the ground. He kicked his legs forward, landed at a run and hurried to a slight decline leading into the forest and into a ravine where black, twisted roots poked from the dirt walls.

"We're out of line of sight from the camp's IR mast," Cha'ril said. "Pigeon up."

A cylinder popped straight up off her back. A clear balloon inflated and carried the cylinder aloft, where it would send a data packet back to the camp and to Gideon, once it caught sight of the camp's communication tower, and relay any waiting messages back to her. The pigeon would disintegrate soon after and vanish like dust in the wind.

Roland continued through the ravine, his rotary cannons angled up and scanning back and forth for any threats that might appear along the edges.

"This is not a mission for us," Cha'ril said. "We are armor. We are not designed for subtlety or stealth. This is a job for Path Finders or Strike Marines."

"I didn't see either of those teams back at the camp," Roland said.

Cha'ril squawked something in Dotari and Roland decided against asking for a translation. He slowed as the ravine began to level off.

"There's a clearing just ahead," Cha'ril said. "Behind a mountain spur. Would be an ideal spot for a landing zone and resupply point as a decent pilot could fly the valley and stay hidden."

"Can't ever fault your ability to read terrain," he said. Roland swung his rotary cannon around to check the canyon edge behind them and caught a glimpse of movement. A black cube arced into the air and fell toward the ravine floor.

"Contact." Roland reached a fist back and rammed it into the dirt wall, swinging the power of his hip and shoulder actuators into the blow. The wall crumbled and a black-clad figure came tumbling down in the avalanche. Roland caught the man by the neck, lifting him out of the dirt and into the air. The legionnaire struggled, kicking at Roland's arm like a fish on a line.

He felt a thump against his torso.

"Don't." The word came from the top of the ravine. Roland swung his rotary cannons around but couldn't find the speaker.

"Roland…" Cha'ril sent him an image capture of a cone attached to his armor, angled straight at his womb. "I've got two on me."

"You kill him and it'll end badly for you," echoed through the ravine. "You try and remove those spikes, it'll end bad too. How about we talk and no one dies?"

"We walked right into an ambush," Cha'ril said. "I'm not aware of any viable options. You?"

Roland lowered the legionnaire so his feet touched the ground but kept his grip around the man's neck. He switched on his speakers.

"We can talk," Roland said. "Just know my finger servos are a bit twitchy. This one won't like what happens if my system goes down."

Another legionnaire walked out to the end of the ravine, a rifle and a thick cylinder wrapped in leather slung over his back, hands up with a detonator in his grip. He came down the slope, skidding across loose pebbles as he approached to within a few yards of Roland.

"I'm Major Aiza," he said. "That's Sergeant Jaso you've got there. I'm willing to drop those spikes if you'll let him go."

"You've got more men around us. Who have more spikes," Roland said.

"And you've got enough firepower to turn this forest into matchsticks," Aiza said. "Let's treat each other with a bit of professional courtesy, eh?"

Aiza opened his grip on the detonator and the spikes on the Dragoons' armor detached with a pop.

Roland mashed a heel against the device, crushing it into scrap, then released his hold on Jaso. The legionnaire went to the fan of loose dirt that was once part of the ravine wall and dug out his gauss rifle. Aiza cocked his head to one side and Jaso jogged back up the slope and ducked around a tree trunk.

"I am Third Lieutenant Cha'ril. By order of the Terran Union, you and your men are to be detained for desertion." Her rotary cannon slowly swept across the top of the ravine.

"I've never sworn an oath to the Union. Never served in your armies. Can't see how you're in any place to give me orders. The other one a Dotari too?" Aiza asked.

"My name is Roland. I don't know your history, but there is blood between the Union and the Ibarras and you're wearing my enemy's colors."

Aiza grabbed his helmet and lifted it off. He looked to be in his late thirties, with dark eyes that hadn't seen sleep in days and a fair stubble across a heavyset jaw. He had a tattoo beneath his left eye that read AB NEG.

"Don't mean to be your enemy. Not my mission to scrap with the Union today. Maybe tomorrow. But if you came looking for a fight, we'll give you one. Something tells me that's not why you're out here."

"The Kesaht have prisoners," Roland said. "Have you found them?"

"We have," Aiza said. "It's a gift from the Saint that you arrived when you did. Come, I'll show you."

Within his womb, Roland's hands clenched into fists and his armor followed suit. This Aiza must have spoken of Saint Kallen. If the Ibarrans venerated her too…Roland forced the implications out of his mind and followed Aiza up the slope.

"Roland, I made a detailed voice and face scan of this Aiza to search against the Union's personnel database, but I doubt we'll find him," Cha'ril sent him over IR.

"I'm certain he's a proccie...and a new one. This means the Ibarras escaped with procedural-generation tubes."

"The Ibarras have a source of tailor-made manpower...and they've had it for years," she said.

"All way above our pay grade. Stay frosty. I trust them about as far as I can throw them."

"He weighs roughly two hundred pounds. With a full recruitment of your armor's servos, you could throw him—"

"Focus. Cha'ril. Focus."

Aiza led them through the woods, where more legionnaires appeared, all larger than most Strike Marines and Rangers Roland had ever come across. The Ibarran troops moved with practiced ease and formed a perimeter around the major and the armor, keeping their weapons pointed away from the two suits.

Roland raised his rotary cannon's barrels to the sky but didn't lock it in place.

"What are you doing on Oricon?" Roland asked.

"The admiral ordered my cohort to defend the civilians from the Kesaht. Here we are. I take it they sent you down with less information," the major said. "Not a surprise. The Kesaht ionized the atmosphere in their initial attack. We're not sure how they do it, but it'll fade in a few days."

"You've fought them before?" Cha'ril asked.

Aiza looked up at her, his face grim.

"Of all the Terran soldiers, I thought they would trust armor with the truth." Aiza slid down a slight depression where a legionnaire manned a command post covered by active camouflage tarps.

Roland got a good look at the cylinder on Aiza's back. The leather straps wrapped up and down the length and a studded metal end cap didn't resemble any military equipment he'd ever seen before. It looked like a hilt missing the blade, but far too large for even the oversized Ibarrans to wield.

"You need to see this." Aiza lifted a holo-screen base out of the command post and held it up for the armor to see: a dozen large sheds at the base of a hyperloop pillar, surrounded by a fence of gleaming red lasers. Stoop-shouldered Rakka patrolled inside on both sides of the fence in groups of seven.

A taller alien ambled between the buildings, passing into full view for a moment, revealing a centaur body with a tail, the tip covered in spikes. It carried a long rifle propped against a shoulder.

"I've seen at least two Sanheel," said the legionnaire in the command post.

"Any Ixio?" Aiza asked.

"No, but they wouldn't be this close to the fighting," the other Ibarran said.

"You want to bring us up to speed?" Roland asked.

"Kesaht are a collective," Aiza said. "Three distinct species—that we know of—working together. Rakka are little more than foot soldiers— we've never seen them do anything but grunt work. Horse-looking sons a bitches are the Sanheel. Officer caste. We've had some success interrogating a few prisoners but haven't been able to learn much. Third are the Ixio, can't say they're the ones in charge. We've observed them and the Sanheel interacting, doesn't seem like one group answers fully to the other."

"What do they want with human prisoners?" Cha'ril asked.

"This is the first time they've taken anyone alive," Aiza said.

"You've found them? The missing?" Roland asked.

The holo screen changed to an infrared view. The glow of human adults sitting shoulder to shoulder bled through the walls of the sheds.

"Can't tell how many more are inside," Aiza said. "They're inside a robotics encampment. Workers from Tonopah do maintenance, run logistics from there. They move the whole thing every couple days, keep pace with the construction."

"The walls aren't hardened." Cha'ril hefted the cannons mounted on her forearm. "One gauss round will tear through the whole place like it was made of tissue paper."

"Which makes an assault a problem," Aiza said.

"There must be fifty of those Rakka, and that one officer we saw looks heavily armed," Cha'ril said. "There are only six of you."

"I had eight until a few days ago. We did our part well enough." Aiza gave the holo projector back to the man in the command post and slung his oversized gauss rifle off his shoulder. "Rakka aren't much of a problem, so long as you aren't dealing with too many at once. Sanheel, though, they've got shields that can take a fair amount of punishment." He gave his rifle a pat.

"You've killed them before," Cha'ril said.

"Set your gauss cannons to an offset double shot. Should break through in one salvo. We lost a lot of lives before we learned that," Aiza said.

"You expect us to work with you to save the civilians?" Cha'ril asked. "For all you know, our fleets are destroying each other in orbit and whatever other forces you have on the ground are dead or in custody."

"I know my duty," Aiza said. "What the admiral orders will be done. I cannot return to her and announce that I held back when I could have accomplished my mission. I thought those from Mars would understand this."

"We are armor. We do not fail," Roland said. "If you are here to find the lost civilians, then we are with you."

"And afterwards?" Aiza asked.

"If you still want to fight, we can. Otherwise, I'd just as soon forget that we ever found you," Roland said.

"'Forget'?" Cha'ril sent him over IR. *"How can you forget? You're talking to him right now. Is this some human negotiation tactic—"*

"Not. Now."

"We can hash it out…later," Aiza said. "My men and I can give you covering fire as you approach. But with the amount of infantry they've got, I don't know how much—"

"We're not going to charge in face-first," Roland said. "We're not going to risk you crunchies missing a shot and punching a hole through five buildings and everyone in between."

"You've got some other way in there you're not telling me about?" Aiza asked.

Roland looked to the columns supporting the hyperloop railway…the eight-story-tall columns.

****

Roland crouched as he walked down the hyperloop tunnel, the sunset's golden light creeping through the occasional gap in side paneling. The view, he decided, was quite nice from this height.

"You've made their job easier," Cha'ril said from just behind him. "We send the ready signal and they blow the support column with a rocket strike. Take out the entire camp full of Kesaht with the rubble. Very efficient use of military munitions."

"Why don't you trust the legionnaires?"

"Why do you? You saw what they did to the *Cairo*. What if that Aiza was the one who killed that turret gunner? Would you be so eager to put yourself up on a target block for him?"

Roland passed into a slight bend, the last marker before they neared the occupied encampment.

"There's something about all of this that's off, Cha'ril. High Command isn't giving us the entire picture. They want us to crush the Ibarrans without question or hesitation, but when we encounter them on our own…they don't act like an enemy."

"I seem to remember two shaped charge explosive devices fastened to my armor. Very friendly."

"Your first Mexican standoff. I'm proud of you." Roland slowed down as heat from the camp showed up on his IR optics. They were a few dozen yards from the camp.

"I don't know what extinct human governments have to do with what happened. But politics, for a moment. You are familiar with the Hale Treaty between Earth and much of the old Alliance?"

"Crucible gate usage and colony-settlement rights. Dull stuff." Roland stopped next to a small concrete placard labeled 137 next to the electromagnetic rail tracks.

"And it specifically forbade the Terran Union from using procedural technology," she said. "All those men down there are living proof of a violation."

Roland gently peeled a tunnel tile away and found a pair of low hills where Aiza was waiting for the armor's signal.

"I'm not certain they're recent proccies," he said. "There are blood tests to confirm that. Telomere length and neuron density that—"

"They are purpose-built for war, Roland. Don't deny it. They're larger, faster, and look a good deal tougher than any crunchy humans I've come across. The Ibarras are making super soldiers. All the billions of proccies created—"

"Born."

"—born before the treaty were little different physically or mentally than a true-born human. That the Ibarras have broken that pattern begs a number of questions."

Roland sent a small camera-tipped probe through a gap in the tunnel wall and confirmed that they were right on top of the column that ran into the middle of the encampment. Climbing up the column farther down the hyperloop line hadn't proven difficult for the armor. Who would repair the damage from their ascent was another concern.

A light blinked twice in between the two hills. He snapped the light at the end of his probe on and off and received the counter-signal, a long flash followed by two brief ones.

"They're in place and ready," Roland said. "You set?"

Cha'ril set her hands against a support beam on the other side of the tunnel.

"What do we do about the Ibarrans when this is over?" she asked.

"If they want to walk away, I won't stop them," he said, turning his helm toward her, "and neither will you."

"'Trust' and 'mercy'...these are not armor words."

His audio sensors picked up the snap of gauss fire, Roland grabbed the metal framework of the tunnel wall and ripped it aside. He ducked through the hole and stepped out onto the top of the column. Below, Rakka around the camp's perimeter fired into the forest. The crack of rifles using chemical propellant sounded through the valley.

"Watch your line of fire." He gripped the edge of the column and swung down, his rail cannon anchor snapped out of his left heel and scraped against the column. Massive fingers in one hand crumbled the column's concrete and he slid down the side.

His targeting computer put threat icons atop every Rakka it made out. Groups of the aliens fell almost simultaneously as the legionnaires fired volleys into the aliens. Guttural commands and pained squeals grew louder as Roland slid closer and closer.

None of the defenders had bothered to look up the column. All were focused on the attack from the surrounding forest—which was precisely what Roland had planned.

A belt-fed machine gun opened up on a shed roof, felling trees with each burst.

Roland checked the distance to the ground…still too far to release without damaging his armor on landing.

"I can take the shot." Cha'ril put a pulsing target icon over the machine-gun nest.

"No, you don't know if any civilians are under it. We're almost—wait…" A group of Rakka stormed out of a maintenance shed, none in full armor but all carried rifles. Roland sheathed his anchor spike and pushed off the wall. His HUD pulsed red warning as he raised his arms up like an eagle about to strike.

He landed on top of two Rakka, crushing them with the crack of bones and a spurt of viscera against the shed walls and the other aliens. Roland backhanded a stunned alien hard enough to send it bouncing across the encampment like a stone skipped across a lake. He spun up his rotary cannons and sent a flurry of bullets up and through the machine-gun position, the angle assured to kill only the aliens, not the human prisoners clustered on the ground floor.

A Rakka fumbled with its rifle next to Roland's knee, so he grabbed it by the arms and hoisted it into the air. It had an upturned nose, red eyes with no trace of an iris, and coarse brown fur on its body between bare skin patches with small nodules. These aliens fastened their armor directly onto their bodies.

Roland whipped the alien against the ground, crushing its spine and skull with a single hit, then stepped out from between the buildings and found the Rakka troops in foxholes firing into the woods around them.

He swung the dead alien back, then hurled it into a post in the laser fence line. The body ignited against the post, sending up a black gout of smoke.

The Rakka near the burning body stopped firing and looked around to see Roland just as his rotary cannon began spinning. The cannon ripped a storm of bullets across the foxholes, shredding the hasty defenses and the Rakka inside to pieces. The rounds buried deep into the ground and any shots that ricocheted or bounced off the aliens' armor went into the woods and away from the sheds.

His cannons wound down as a tall door on one of the sheds behind him burst open, bathing Roland in light. A Sanheel galloped out, its four hooves sparking against the poured concrete slab that ran beneath the entire encampment.

The Sanheel leveled its long rifle at Roland, and he fought the well-trained response to fire with his own gauss cannons. He couldn't shoot yet, not while there were civilians behind the Kesaht officer.

The alien's rifle fired, blasting flechettes across Roland's chest and helmet. His HUD wavered, then blinked off as the optics in his helm went haywire. A blow struck down on his right shoulder, knocking him off-balance and sending his fist scraping against the ground.

Roland struck out blindly and felt his fist connect…then freeze in place. A jolt of energy went up his arm as he pulled it back. He slapped the back of his other hand against his helm and his optics came back online.

He looked up and saw the Sanheel loading a long metal slug into its rifle. Roland stomped the weapon, snapping it in half. The Sanheel opened its jowly mouth and bellowed at him, rows and rows of needle-sharp teeth quivering. Its single eye housed several pupils that fluctuated with color.

It swung the broken rifle like a club at Roland's helm. He caught it easily and dug his fingers into the metal. The Sanheel tugged and shut its mouth as it found the armor's grip quite firm. Roland yanked the club away, then stabbed the end at the previous owner. A force field flared to life, rippling as the rifle butt slid across it.

Then, with an audible pop, the shield collapsed.

Roland grabbed the Sanheel by the upper edge of its breast plate and slammed his helm forward, striking the upper metal edge against the alien's eye. It fumbled back, but Roland kept it close. He slammed a foot onto the Sanheel's forward hoof, then slapped his hands against the side of the alien's head.

Roland ripped its head clean off its shoulders and spiked it against the concrete slab.

The surviving Rakka began hooting. Some crawled out of their foxholes and crawled toward the laser fence.

"Behind you!" Cha'ril called out.

Roland ducked and turned. Another Sanheel, with its rifle pointed right at Roland, galloped around a building. Its shield flared along its flank and its rear legs buckled. Roland thrust his forearm-mounted cannons at the alien and fired. The quick one-two punch of the round ripped through its shields and a gauss shell exploded out of the creature's back. It crumbled forward, leaving a slick of black blood behind it.

The Rakka's hooting grew louder. One reared up and tossed its weapon aside. Roaring, it charged straight for the armor. The rest picked up the cry and swarmed toward Roland.

He booted the first Rakka into the laser wire fence. An alien jumped on his back, scratching at his rail rifle with its claws. Roland bent the elbow of one arm around, plucked the assailant off him and then used it as a club, crushing several of the berserkers with each blow.

A Rakka climbed onto the shoulders of another alien and jumped at Roland. He brought a fist down and hammered it into the pavement.

It took him another thirty bloody seconds to finish off the last of the aliens. Yellow mist rose from the corpses and their flesh melted into ooze, sloughing off skeletons that crumbled into dust moments after exposure to air. Cyborg implants in the alien's skulls overloaded and burnt, looking like lumps of broken coal.

The two Sanheel corpses remained whole. Cha'ril walked up to him, her hands and forearms covered in steaming yellow gunk.

"I took care of the third big one," she said, holding." She held up a severed hand. "I thought it would disintegrate with the others, thought we'd get a gene sample from this." She tossed it against the headless corpse.

"The prisoners…" Roland stepped over the body and into the maintenance building. The upper floor was nothing but half-complete construction drones and auto-assemblers. On the bottom floor were a dozen men and women bound to a long metal chain. The lower half of their heads and necks were covered in a black metal that reflected the building's light like a mirror. All of them gazed up, their eyes unfocused.

"What did they do to them?" Cha'ril asked.

"Don't touch!" A shout came from beyond the laser fence. A gauss rifle snapped and a post broke in half, creating a hole in the fence. Aiza and three of his men charged through the gap. Aiza raised a hand next to his head and pointed forward, and the three split off toward different buildings.

The major hurried past the armor and went to the nearest colonist. He drew a device that looked like a thin metal wand from off his thigh and pressed the tip against the shiny metal on the base of the woman's neck.

"What happened to the Rakka?" Roland asked. "That they'd drop their weapons and come at me with tooth and claw in a rage like that…"

"There's some sort of connection between the Sanheel and the Rakka," the major said. "When the grunts lose all their officers, they revert to some sort of primitive compulsion. Very aggressive. Not so bad when you're armor. It's a bit different when you're in a derelict ship and those piggies are running all over the place."

"You might have told us as much," Cha'ril said. "And you could tell us what you're doing to the hostages."

"I wasn't exactly sure you'd carry out your part of the plan. You had the chance to cut back to town. Didn't want to share anything useful until I saw you were committed. As for our colonists, the

Kesaht have them in compliance collars," Aiza said. "Puts them somewhere between euphoria and sleep. You try and rip them off and you'll kill the wearer."

The collar rippled, then peeled off the prisoner and fell to the floor. The woman blinked hard and tried to rub her eyes. Aiza moved to the next person.

"What in the Sam Hill…" The groggy prisoner looked up at the armor and blinked hard, then turned her gaze to the dead Sanheel and gasped. She tried to scoot away from the body and bumped into the back wall.

"Easy," Aiza said, putting a hand on her shoulder, "you're safe now." He pointed at the chains on her wrists, then to Roland.

"Nothing special about those. You mind?"

The woman lifted her bound hands up to Roland, and he snapped the chain links between the cuffs.

"Thank you," she said. "We were on pylon ninety-nine when those things—"

"Here." Aiza pressed the wand into her

hands. "Hold the tip against the collar until it finds the release frequency. You do the rest." He got to his feet and touched the side of his helmet. It folded back into the ring at the base of his neck. Aiza wore an earpiece, one Roland hadn't seen on him earlier.

"They're not all here," the major said. "Still missing eighteen of them...all children."

"The Kesaht took them somewhere else," Roland said. "We'll find them."

"No." Aiza pointed to another building. "The teacher and the chaperones are in that building. Kids aren't here. We saw a small Kesaht shuttle in the valley a couple hours ago. They must've taken them...and only them. Damn it."

"Where could they be?" Roland asked.

"Anywhere. If their in-atmo craft have a range, we haven't seen it yet. Some kind of anti-grav that..." Aiza cocked his head slightly to one side. "Yes, ma'am...right away."

Roland opened his communications suite and got nothing but static.

"Who are you talking to...and how?" he

asked.

"I'm afraid this is where we leave you," Aiza said. "You send up a pigeon to Tonopah and they'll send a truck to pick everyone up. You can keep the sonic keys, make some of your own." The major backed away, his gaze on the armor.

"What do we say to Gideon if we just let them go?" Cha'ril asked over their IR.

"The truth," Roland said. He switched back to his speakers. "Major. The next time we see each other, the circumstances may be different."

"Aye." Aiza said, looking at the hostages. "That's war. Some days you're the hero." He turned his head to the trail of dead aliens outside the building. "Some days you're the villain. I hope we don't see each other ever again. I doubt it'll end well for either of us."

He put two fingers against his earpiece.

"What's that? As you wish." Aiza set his rifle to the ground, then unsnapped the hilt from his back. He carried it in two hands to Roland, straining against the weight.

"Morrigan wants you to have it." He set the hilt into Roland's hand. "May the Saint bless you and keep you." Aiza thumped a fist against his heart, picked up his rifle, and vanished into the night.

"What's a 'Morrigan'?" Cha'ril asked.

"A name, I think." Roland gripped the hilt in both hands. He touched a button on the forward edge, and a blade snapped out in segments. It locked into a sword far too large for a normal man to wield, but scaled to Roland's size and complete with a simple cross guard. He spun the weapon around and looked at the pommel: a Templar cross with the word "Morrigan" embossed along the edge.

"No…" Cha'ril said. "That's impossible."

"This was designed to be used by armor," Roland said. He set the blade in one hand and examined it closely. The metal was nicked and scratched in several places, and; a yellowish discoloration of Rakka blood marred the forward third.

"This was used in battle…by armor,"

Roland said.

"I thought it was impossible for proccies to get the skull plugs and become armor," Cha'ril said. "How are the Ibarrans creating armor soldiers?"

"I don't think they are." Roland leveled the sword back to Tonopah. "But I know who will have answers."

CHAPTER 9

Lettow adjusted the position of his *Javelin* class artillery ship squadron to just behind a cruiser strike group in his holo tank. He punched in a least distance course to Oricon and double tapped a CONFIRM icon to send the plan to Strickland.

Strickland raised an eyebrow at the admiral.

Lettow pointed at the slow-moving Kesaht fleet, still on course for the Crucible gate. The 14th's projected course and the aliens' would come close to weapons range, too close for Lettow's comfort.

"We come at them with the *Javelins* unsheathed and they may think we're itching for a fight," Lettow said.

He moved the holo tank view back to the slow moving alien fleet. They had twice the number of ships as the 14th, but it was their three battleships that concerned the admiral the most. Each was larger than the *Ardennes*, and boasted cannon turrets on the dorsal and ventral hulls. Enhanced pictures of the ship's surface showed likely torpedo tubes…weapons with warheads and acceleration capabilities that were a mystery to him. Fighting an enemy he didn't know would be like trying to box with a blindfold over his eyes.

"The Ibarrans said the Kesaht attacked the colony," the operations officer said.

"I'm not ready to trust them. We pick a fight with them here and now and there will be a war between Earth and these new aliens, one the Ibarrans will have started for us. This is why I hate first contact missions," Lettow said.

"Understood…Commander Rusk reports the Crucible is clear of all explosive devices, anticipates full functionality in twenty-six hours. We could access the gate to leave in twelve."

"Twenty-six hours until anyone else can arrive," Lettow said. "Plenty of time for things to play out. Signal the fleet. We weigh anchor in two minutes for Oricon."

Lettow went to his command chair and strapped himself in as the *Ardennes* went to ready alert. He snapped on his helmet and double checked his air supply. The bridge switched to local IR as the atmosphere drained out through the vents and the ship lurched forward as the engines flared to life.

He pulled up a screen from his chair arm and watched as his fleet reformed into a hemisphere with the *Ardennes,* strike carriers *Gettysburg* and *Falklands,* the *Javelin* artillery ships and support craft behind the screen of cruisers, frigates, and destroyers.

"Sir," Strickland said from his seat to the admiral's right, "just detected a change from the Kesaht fleet. They're accelerating."

On his screen, the time projection on the alien vessels' arrival to the Crucible shortened to less than a day.

"We're being hailed by the Kesaht," the communications officer said. "It's coming over the first contact frequencies we tried earlier."

"So they can speak," Lettow said. "Guess we gave them a reason to talk. Put it through."

He raised the arm with his screen up and locked it in place in front of his face. The screen flickered, then resolved into one of the ugliest aliens Lettow had ever seen. Its skull was a rounded cone, with a bulldog's jaw buffered by coarse hair and jet black eyes. Data cables ran out of the back of its head and into red and gold armor on its shoulders.

The alien huffed, turning its head slightly from side to side as it examined Lettow.

"I am Primus Gor'thig, risen Sanheel of the Kesaht Hegemony," the alien said in decent English. "We pursued one of your fleets to this system to punish them for attacking one of our worlds. The blood debt has been paid, now we demand safe and unhindered passage through the Crucible gate."

Lettow kept his face neutral as he considered the alien's words.

"I am unaware of any such attack," Lettow said. Indeed, what the alien just said directly contradicted the story the Ibarran admiral gave him. "To the best of my knowledge, this is the first time the Terran Union has ever encountered your species."

"Is the other fleet not full of your kind?" Gor'thig asked. "Your ships are of the same shape. You look like them."

"That fleet is not of the Terran Union; they stand apart from us. But the colony on Oricon *is* part of the Terran Union. What happens to the innocent people down there is very much my concern and you need to end your communication jamming and explain your aggression against a colony full of builders."

"Your kind are fractured, squabbling? This is not a weakness the Kesaht Hegemony suffers. We are many races, all working toward a common good. I do not understand how humans can operate independently of each other."

"I'm not asking you to understand. There will be time for the Terran Union and your Hegemony to engage in diplomatic efforts later…after you tell me what's happened to Oricon," Lettow said.

"The not-Terran-but-Terran fleet landed soldiers on the moon," Gor'thig said. "I sent troops to find them and bring me their skins. Your soldiers massacred a Kesaht research team. Blood must follow blood."

"The Ibarrans are not of the Union, but if you've killed civilians, then—"

"We do not murder those without blood on their hands. We seek only to balance the scales. The atmosphere ionization will dissipate in two rotations of the moon. I assume denying an enemy the ability to communicate is a human tactic."

An icon flashed on Lettow's screen. One of the Kesaht battleships had broken off from the fleet and was on course to Oricon.

"I will remove my troops from the moon,"

Gor'thig said. "We bled the Terran-not-Terran fleet while the hunt on the ground went on. The scales are balanced. Once I have them back, we will leave this system. Do not get in our way."

The channel closed.

Lettow sat for a moment, processing. First contact scenarios were one of the toughest a commander could face. Without knowing the culture and diplomatic ways of these Kesaht, one misstep could send these new aliens into the arms of Earth's enemies, or bring them over as new allies.

He'd been on the rescue mission that answered the distress call from the *Belisarius*; he knew just how bad first contact could turn out.

"Comms, we need contact with Oricon," Lettow said. "If they slaughtered the colonists, they'll learn how the Terran Union answers a blood debt."

"We're still trying, admiral," the lieutenant said. "Whatever they did to the atmosphere is scrambling any and all communication waveforms. I've got the signals section on every ship working on it."

"It's not like we can send up a smoke signal," Strickland said. "Or even a…wait, we're another hour from Auburn City, coming into view as the moon rotates. Comms, do you still learn Morse code and how to use Aldis lamps at Officer's Candidate School?"

"Yes, sir. The signal lamps are one of our backup communication channels."

"We can see the surface just fine," Lettow said. "If the armor's made it to the city, they know we're here and we're on the way."

"They should be looking for us," Strickland said. "Our targeting cameras could spot a dog taking a leak on a mesquite bush outside of Phoenix from Mars."

"Figure out a way to make a signal obvious enough for them to notice," the admiral said to the red-faced comms officer.

"Aye aye," he said.

"What that Gor'thig said doesn't match the Ibarrans' story," Strickland said. "But if they were on the run after raiding the Kesaht, I doubt that Admiral Faben would come clean."

"We're all playing each other," Lettow said. "The Ibarrans are after something and are running the clock until they find it. I have a hard time buying Gor'thig's noble warrior routine. He didn't contact us until we forced his hand. And I'm juggling if we should engage the Kesaht, run down the Ibarrans or go help the colony that might not need any assistance at all.

"We stay the course until we can see Auburn city with our own eyes. Then I'll know our next move." The admiral interlaced his fingers and watched as Oricon turned.

CHAPTER 10

Roland and Cha'ril flanked the gate through the hasty barricade around Tonopah as the trucks full of rescued colonists drove through. Roland looked over the wall and was certain every last person in the town was pressed around the gate.

"They left the watch towers unmanned," Cha'ril said to Roland over closed IR.

"We're watching for them. You think there are any more Kesaht out here?"

"It is a distinct possibility," she said. "Haven't heard the sound of gauss cannons from Gideon or Aignar. If they haven't found and eliminated any stragglers, the town is under threat. The legionnaires led off a significant number of enemy foot soldiers. I doubt they killed them all."

"If there were any survivors, they were smart enough not to engage us on the way back to town. Doubt they'd stand a better chance attacking this fortified location." Roland grabbed the top of the metal barricade and managed to shake it back and forth with ease.

"Improved location," he said.

"Hey!" Dinkins waved up at Roland. "Where are the children? Did you find the children?"

"No sign of them," Roland said.

Dinkins' shoulders drooped. He slunk down to the ground and buried his face in the crook of his arm.

"Tim! Tim!" His wife Sally came out of the gate, dragging a woman in her late early twenties by the hand.

"Maria, tell the foreman what you told me." Sally clung to her arm. "And the armor, hurry!"

"I'm the head of child education." She looked up at Roland with a blank expression. She, like many of the others the armor rescued, was on the verge of shock. "Everyone just calls me the school marm. But I was with the kids when the aliens took us. They separated me from the children near one of their shuttles. They didn't take George or Vinnie Tate; they're the oldest boys we have. Thirteen and fifteen."

"You saw the children loaded into the shuttle?" Cha'ril asked.

Maria nodded.

"They could be anywhere," Roland said.

"But they're alive." Dinkins wiped tears away and got back onto his feet.

"Not necessar—" Cha'ril stopped when Roland's helm snapped up at her. "Of course they're alive."

"What can you do?" Sally asked. "Can you track them or—"

"We don't fly," Roland said. "But there may be a way to find them. Do you have anyone with xeno-tech or biology experience?"

"We've got…" Dinkins looked at his wife

and frowned. She snapped her fingers and ran back into the town. "We've got a former Path Finder. He's still got his old rig too. Why do you ask?"

Cha'ril reached behind her back and tossed a black plastic sack onto the ground. A Sanheel head rolled out and stopped in the middle of the road. Severed data cables twitched in its skull sockets like Medusa at the end of her tail. The alien's eyes were rolled back into its head, tongue impaled on a fang.

Maria screamed and ran back inside.

"Oops," Cha'ril said.

Dinkins shuffled back and bumped into the back of a truck.

"How did you-you-you…" the foreman stammered.

"The Sanheels' bodies disintegrate just like the Rakka," Cha'ril said. "But if you rip their heads off before they die, that part tends to stick around."

"What? What?" Johannsen the sniper pushed through the crowd, clutching a slightly larger than normal gauntlet to his chest. Sally was right behind him, pushing him along.

"What is the damn hurry—Holy shit!" Johannsen almost stumbled over the alien's head. He jumped over it like the ground was electrified. "A little warning? Huh?" He glared at Sally.

"You were a Path Finder?" Roland asked.

"That's right. Eight years." Johannsen removed his jacket and slipped his hand into his gauntlet. "Did bio surveys on twenty-three different worlds." He kicked the side of the alien's head.

"I'm used to looking at these through a scope. Christ, they're ugly." He went to one knee and passed the lit fingertips of his gauntlet over the head.

"Aesthetics aside," Cha'ril said, "what can you tell us about it? The implants are highly unusual for any encountered species."

Johannsen drew a small wand from his gauntlet and stuck it into the Sanheel's cheek. He dabbed a bit of flesh into a tiny receptacle, then forced the tip into the flesh around a data cable and pushed it deeper until it touched the skull.

"Before these Kesaht showed up, I would

have told you there wasn't a single cyborg species in the galaxy. Might be some that need prosthetic replacements, but to see such extensive work done on a soldier…never," Johansson said.

"Why's that?" Roland asked.

"The Xaros. They'd hack anything with a CPU. One drone gets near this big pile of shit and he'd be shut down or turn on his buddies at the drone's order. The Qa'Resh never, ever recruited a species that couldn't survive without augmentation. Waste of time, no way they could fight the Xaros. Path Finders might find the occasional species that might develop intelligence on an old Xaros-occupied world, or we'd bump into another Alliance species that was scoping out the same planets we were." His gauntlet beeped.

"What have we here?" Johannsen squinted at his screen. "Carbon based…normal male female profile in the DNA…not a match for anything in the database. And—that's funny. There's another species' DNA in here." He tapped the data wire touching his probe wand.

"Inside his head?" Cha'ril asked.

"No, inside the wires. Looks like another alien built the cables that're in his brain box," Johannsen said, tapping his gauntlet, then looking up at the armor. "You guys have some of the same thing, right?" He touched the base of his skull.

"Our plugs make us armor," Cha'ril said. "Our implants form a biological computer joined to the armor's systems. That's why the Xaros could never affect armor during the war. These Sanheel augmentations seem drastically different."

"Brain structure is largely similar for mammalian species, especially ones that developed upright, two legs or not. The implants this one has are mostly in the speech and hearing centers. What I'm assuming are the speech and hearing parts. There's a lot of hardware in there."

"The Rakka do not seem sophisticated enough to perform this level of augmentation," Cha'ril said. "Perhaps there is a higher order of the Rakka."

"Now that is unusual." Johannsen rubbed an

eye. "There's a 3% match between the two species. It would have to come from interbreeding—which my entire understanding of xeno biology says is impossible—or a common ancestor. A very distant ancestor."

"They're from the same planet?" Roland asked. "Earth had several kinds of hominids at one time."

"We're a lot closer to Cro-Magnon man than this guy is to whoever wired him," Johansson said. "If only the Rakka didn't melt after we killed them."

"How much of a sample do you need?" Roland offered his forearm to Johannsen, where black blood stained the armor up to the elbow.

Johannsen balked for a moment, then rubbed another wand along the dried viscera.

"I'm really…glad you guys are on our side," he said. "Never thought I'd get back in the swing of biology again."

"Why'd you leave the Path Finders?" Roland asked.

"Dodging mega fauna and carnivorous plants for years on end gets a bit old," he said. "My term was up, had the chance to settle a garden world like this one and watch my kids grow up…" He looked aside for a moment, his eyes unfocused. He shook his head quickly and went back to his gauntlet.

"You have a missing child?" Cha'ril asked.

"Jessica. I need to focus," Johannsen said.

"You're helping us to find her," Roland said. "Until we know more about these Kesaht, we're in the dark trying to tell what an elephant looks like just by touching a leg."

"What is an elephant?" Cha'ril asked.

Johansson shook his head at the screen. "This can't be right. DNA has zero percent match with the other two strands. I'd say this came from a completely different star system."

"There's an alien race we haven't encountered yet," Cha'ril said.

"And they're the ones wiring up the Sanheel and the Rakka," Roland said.

Dinkins walked out of the gate and gave the Sanheel head a wide berth. He held a ruggedized data slate in one hand, antennae as long as his forearm stuck from the top.

"We're picking up some weak transmissions from space," the foreman said. "Your fleet, I take it. If the scrambling's fading away, then the tracker unit might start working. But…" He slapped the side.

"The colonists have trackers? Now you tell us?" Cha'ril asked.

"Doesn't matter when they're not working. Things have been crazy the last few days. Give me a break, okay?" Dinkins said. "I thought your armor might have a signal booster. The units are offline until they get a ping. Privacy laws still apply out here. They're meant to find people after avalanches, cave-ins, little kids lost in the woods…"

Roland scanned through his open frequencies. There was a faint signal that washed in and out, like trying to eavesdrop on a conversation during a windy day.

"The interference is still too strong," he said. "But keep trying."

A faint echo of gauss cannons rumbled down the valley.

Cha'ril raised her forearm weapon and chambered rounds from her ammo line.

"Gideon and Aignar," she said.

"Get your militia on the walls," Roland said. "We're going to help them."

"Can't you stay here and help us?" Dinkins asked.

"We let them get within range and you'll take casualties," Roland said. "We are armor. We attack." He pointed a finger at the sniper that nearly killed him earlier.

"I said I was sorry. Get over it." Johannsson shrugged. "And it won't happen again. Path Finder's honor."

Treads unfolded from the armors' legs and they rolled out.

****

Gideon banged a fist against the side of his forearm cannons. A Rakka bullet had hit the feeder line where it joined the weapon and the shells weren't loading properly. He stood up from behind a boulder and let off a quick burst from his rotary gun into a copse of trees at the base of the mountainside where he took cover.

The bullets felled trees and the return fire that sprang off the boulder assured him that the Kesaht were still hot on his heels.

"Aignar?" Gideon sent over IR.

"I've got one," Aignar said. "Working the base with my anchor now."

Gideon dashed to another tall rock. Bullets from the Rakka sprang off his legs and bit into the dirt around him. He kept running past the next chance for cover. The boulder exploded as a Sanheel spike tore through.

He thrust his cannon arm towards the enemy and got off two shots before the line jammed again. He slid down an embankment as enemy fire spat through the dirt over his head. The bullets careened off stones in a creek bed.

"You have your exfil set?" Gideon asked.

"You know how close they are to you, sir? Pushing in five…"

Gideon hurried up the steep slope and offered a decent target to the Rakka and Sanheel charging at him into a draw buffeted by two mountain slopes. One of the three Sanheel spotted him and charged forward, trampling more than one Rakka that was too slow to get out of the way. As the other Sanheel galloped after the leader, they raised long rifles over their heads and bellowed a war cry.

"Rook rook! Rook rook!" echoed off the mountainsides.

The Sanheel broke ahead of the Rakka, closing on Gideon, where he had his back against a wall.

There was a crack of thunder. A boulder broke loose from the steep cliffs against the forest where the aliens were. The Mule-sized rock crashed against the slope and knocked loose another rock, and another. A landslide barreled down, shaking the ground hard enough that Gideon felt the vibration through his womb.

On the mountainside, where the initial rock had been, Aignar hurried away from the gaping wound.

The Rakka saw their doom coming right for them. They panicked, pushing against each other and trying to run in every direction.

The three Sanheel, however, galloped faster, straight toward Gideon.

The rock slide hit the forest and obliterated it, crushing the Rakka into paste. The Sanheel outpaced the destruction, keeping just ahead like they were running from an incoming tide at the beach.

One of the Sanheel aimed his rifle at Gideon, who threw himself to the side as the heavy bolt struck the side of the draw and blew soil and shards of rock around him. Gideon heard another long rifle boom, but the shot wasn't for him.

He charged out of the ravine. Aignar was still struggling along the mountainside, an easy and obvious target for the Sanheel. One took careful aim at the armor.

"You're not done with me!" Gideon shouted. He ripped his damaged ammo line out of his gauss cannons and pulled an ammo box out from beneath his back armor. His HUD flashed a warning as he ran forward, processed target information on the three aliens, and manually loaded his gauss cannons. The neural load on his brain was dangerously close to crossing the redline and destroying his mind.

He tasted blood in his mouth and fumbled with the ammo box. He spun the rotary gun on his shoulder and set it to fire blind. Bullets peppered the Sanheel, all bouncing off their shields. One of the aliens slapped another on the shoulder and pointed at him. The alien slid a pilum-sized bullet into his rifle's breach. Gideon slid to a stop as the Sanheel aiming at Aignar adjusted his aim.

Gideon swept his rotary gun toward the long

rifle, his bullets shattered the forward third. The centaur flung the rifle away in surprise. Gideon stitched bullets across the shield of the Sanheel about to shoot him, and struck it on the wrist where it reached through the shield to steady the weapon.

Gideon's rotary gun kept spinning, the ammo supply exhausted. He finally slammed the gauss magazine home and racked the manual slide.

He shot the Sanheel nursing a bleeding and broken wrist in the chest. The impact against the shield pushed it back and into its fellow, the last one with a functional long rifle. The one with the rifle shoved his way into the open and leveled his weapon at Gideon from the hip.

The armor shot at the Sanheel's face, the flash of the shields blocking the alien's sight. The alien fired anyway and the ground erupted just in front of Gideon. A cloud of dust washed over the three aliens.

The one with the broken wrist picked up its rifle, pointed ears tipped with acoustic sensors perking up as a shadow emerged from the dust.

Gideon punched his cannon arm against the thick armor plates of the Sanheel's stomach. He fired both barrels and blew the alien's back out. He shoved the falling corpse against the second as it swung its rifle like a club. The rifle hit Gideon's arm and knocked the magazine off and sent it spinning through the air.

Gideon hooked a punch with his right arm and the Sanheel caught his fist with both hands. The alien pushed against the fist and was barely able to match the armor's strength. Gideon angled his gauss cannons at the Sanheel's face.

"Still have two in the chamber," he said and blew the alien's head into an expanding cloud of hair, teeth, and eyeballs.

The last reared up and struck Gideon with his front hooves. The twin blows hit with a *whack*, leaving dents in Gideon's breast plate. He stumbled back, nearly tripping over one of the bodies.

The Sanheel jammed its forelegs against the ground, then spun its back haunches around to buck Gideon.

The armor ducked beneath the metal-shod hooves, then reached up and grabbed the Sanheel by the ankles. He twisted around and slammed the alien against the ground like a sack of flour. He grabbed his stunned opponent by the neck and pulled a fist back. Locking two fingers forward, he stabbed them through its eyes. He crushed its front skull, clenching his hand into a fist and ripped backwards. Gray matter and sparking cyborg parts oozed from between his fingers.

Gideon tossed the mess aside and went to find his gauss magazine.

"Sir?" Aignar slid down the mountainside, leaving a trail of dust behind him.

"What made you think you could exfiltrate along the side of a mountain?" Gideon tapped the magazine against the side of his helm to knock dust out of it, then slammed it into his cannon. "In the open."

"They were right on top of you," Aignar said. "It was either find a perfect solution two minutes too late or do something constructive right away." Aignar motioned back to the jumble of rocks, trees, and Rakka. A yellow haze from the rapidly decaying bodies rose from the rubble.

"I've been through worse ambushes," Gideon said.

He kicked a Sanheel corpse as the flesh melted away. The ivory white of bare skull flaked into dust within seconds of contact with the air.

"Roland and Cha'ril." Aignar raised an arm and waved to the other pair on the far end of the landslide.

"Lieutenant, we…found…—opah," Roland's tortured IR transmission barely came through.

"We'll never get anything at this rate." Gideon stretched his arms out to the side, then clapped them over his head in long and short beats, sending the Morse code for R-T-B. Return to base.

The other pair of armor transformed to their travel mode and rolled away.

"As the frog hops," Aignar nodded at the field of rubble, then looked to the mountains between them and Tonopah, "or as the crow flies?"

"The mountains. No more avalanches."

"Fine by me," Aignar said.

****

Gideon held the Templar sword and ran fingers down the blood groove. The rest of his lance stood in a circle with him. The Tonopah workers and family members clustered around two hauler trucks, helping former prisoners out of the dusty ore beds.

"Impressive construction," he said. "A graphenium lattice inside the blade. Should be as hard to destroy as our armor."

"Do you know the name—'Morrigan'?" Roland asked.

"I don't." Gideon clicked the button on the hilt and the blade collapsed into it. He gripped it tightly for a moment, then handed it back to Roland.

"Then the Ibarras are making their own armor," Cha'ril said.

"I doubt that," Gideon said. "The Corps and Dr. Eeks tried long and hard to find a way to create a proccie that could take the plugs. The results were…tragic. Proccie neural pathways are too weak to take the plugs—which is to be expected when you create a mind in a computer while the body grows over the course of nine days. This Morrigan, she's either a new recruit from Ibarra's traitors or…"

"She was armor that defected with them," Roland said.

"Armor Corps isn't that big," Aignar said. "The lieutenant should know that name, right, sir?"

"We had a spy active in the Ibarra camp until a few months ago," Gideon said. "The spy said there were some…changes to the armor that went with her. We didn't get much more than that, but it fit with what else the spy sent back. The Ibarras didn't keep the Terran military and social structure after they left. They reformed with Marc and Stacey Ibarra as their supreme leaders, unquestioned loyalty, all of it borderline fanaticism."

"How many went with the Ibarras?" Cha'ril asked.

"All the survivors from 3rd Squadron's fight against the Haesh and a few others," Gideon said.

"I thought 3rd Squadron was listed as missing in action along with…" Aignar touched a hand to his helm's jawline. "…High Command lied to us. They don't want the public knowing that armor can be anything but the heroic statues people think of in Memorial Square."

"They are the Armor Corps' shame." Gideon pointed at Roland. "If you encounter them, you will *not* make friends. Combat conditions be damned. You bring them back for General Laran to deal with. Dead or alive. Am I clear?"

"Crystal, sir." Roland brought the hilt down to his leg, where it mag-locked against his thigh.

Over the horizon, a dozen Mule and Destrier transports, flanked by fighter escorts, flew toward Tonopah.

"Fleet managed to get a few relay satellites into orbit. Captain Sobieski's ordered the town evacuated," Gideon said. "We're going back to Auburn to link up with the rest of the company. Get to the air pad and box up. It'll be cramped."

CHAPTER 11

Petty Officer Juanita Ruiz plugged her gauntlet into a data core and opened a diagnostics program. The *Ardennes'* master computer had detected an "anomaly" and her section leaders decided that she, of all people, had to climb down into the stacks and check the problem. This was part and parcel of her normal duties, but doing it while the ship was at battle stations—and on the verge of a potential fight—was not how she wanted to spend her evening.

The stacks were cramped and sectioned off from the rest of the ship. If the *Ardennes* took damage while she was in here…she shivered.

Trying and failing to forget stories about crew trapped inside stricken ships waiting for rescue while their air supply dwindled to nothing.

A screen on the data stack blinked on and requested her personal access code.

"That's odd." She ran the diagnostic again and got an error buzzer in her ear. "Did we get a firmware update?" She shrugged and tapped in her code.

A word popped up on the screen: PRIPET. The letters seethed with color. Ruiz froze, her jaw went slack, and her eyes refused to blink. More words: CESTUS. SPARROW. BARON.

Ruiz regained control of her faculties. She looked around for a moment, confused as to where she was. Text formed on the screen, outlining instructions and ending with a list of names. She committed it all to memory and wiped the data buffers.

She knew what to do, and she knew it was right down to the core of her being.

****

Aignar sat on a bundle of steel beams on the outer edge of Tonopah's lone air pad. He had his right bottom leg in his lap. The armor slab that covered the limb's tread and mechanical housing was open, and he held a too small tool in his massive hands, picking at flakes of rock and plant matter mashed into his gears. Two links of broken treads sat between him and Cha'ril, who was sitting next to him and doing the same repairs to his other lower leg.

Across the tarmac, Gideon and Roland organized the townsfolk into lines for the evacuation that was on the way.

"I hate breaking track," Aignar said, "the bane of armor since the First World War."

"You know the treads are more likely to break under sheering forces," she said. "Which is why that fact was pounded into us during training. I seem to recall us doing these exact same repairs after a field exercise in the Himalayas."

"We were fixing Roland's treads, not mine." Aignar leaned forward and moved his incomplete legs around. "Huh, I can still feel them. Phantom limb syndrome from an amputee while inside incomplete armor. Dr. Eeks would have a field day with this."

"Is there an error with your plugs?" Cha'ril yanked a branch dripping with sap from Aignar's leg and tossed it aside.

"System's fine. Just a side effect of being incomplete in both bodies," Aignar said.

"It is unfortunate that your body rejects replacement organs," she said. "Dotari medical science cannot replace our limbs with near perfect replicas. Most Dotari so injured opt for cybernetics that can almost pass for the real thing. But out of armor, you use prosthetics that are almost…"

"Crude," Aignar said. "The better stuff has to tap directly into my nerve endings. I do that and my synch rating in armor will suffer. Badly. But I can get around just fine. It's not like I'm a pirate with peg legs and hooks for hands."

"If there was some breakthrough that would make you whole, would you take it? Even if it cost you your armor?" she asked.

"There's no such thing," he snapped. "Wondering about some magic transformation is a waste of time. If my aunt had balls, she'd be my uncle. But since you asked, no I wouldn't give up my armor for anything. You know what happened to Saint Kallen? She was diagnosed with Batten's Disease, could've left the Iron Hearts behind, gone into treatment and survived. She chose to keep fighting, knowing the decision was a death sentence. How could I punch out from you and the others just to walk around like some sort of…normal person?"

"The plugs in the base of our skulls mark us out as anything but normal," she said. "We give up so much to be armor."

"But in return…" He held up his lower leg and the ankle servo jerked from side to side. "Always a lot more glamorous in the movies."

"Aignar, you have a child. How is being

armor affecting you as a parent?"

"Damn, Cha'ril. I should be on a shrink's couch for that kind of a question."

"I don't want you to become any smaller," she said. "If the question bothers you, then—"

"Ask me the real question. You're beating around the bush." He dug his tool into the ankle housing and scraped thorn branches out onto the ground. "And speaking of bushes…"

"Human soldiers do not become pregnant while they're on active duty. I am aware of the birth control measures your females go through. But what would happen if one does become pregnant?"

"Shipped off the front lines, that's for sure," Aignar said. "Can't have a baby that close to danger. And it's not like a woman with a bun in the oven is that effective on the front lines. My ex, when she was about to pop Joshua, could barely pick up anything. Then it was, 'Rub my feet' this, 'I'm so uncomfortable' that…I was in the field for most of the pregnancy. Pretty sure that was a contributing factor to the divorce. Among other things."

"Such a conflict…I have trouble understanding it. Dotari lay a single egg after a brief gestation period. Traditionally, the grandparents will care for the egg until it hatches, then the mother will provide lactation. I'm surprised humans manage so well with only two nipples—"

"Skip ahead before you start talking about your cloaca."

"A pregnant Dotari is not removed from combat," she said. "All our ships carry crèches and eggs are transported back to our home world as soon as possible. The hatching can be delayed until the mother's tour of duty is complete."

"Interesting."

"Did you feel any pressure to procreate after the Ember War? When there were so few humans left?"

"I was a kid when that happened. My procreation urge came after too many beers and being on my honeymoon. No one ever told me I had to have kids, not like there weren't proccie tubes churning out new people every nine days. If the Hale Treaty hadn't shut down the proccies, we'd have more people in the Solar System than right before the Xaros showed up."

"In Dotari history, there was an accident aboard the *Canticle of Reason*, the colony fleet's flag ship. Tens of thousands lost in a day. The Council of Firsts decided that every Dotari woman of laying age would have their birth control measures removed."

"They forced women to have babies?"

"Hardly. Dotari females have a hormonal need for procreation—not as life-threatening as what the Karigole deal with—but the urge is so strong that it does not require alcohol and honey from Luna to consummate. The Council just lets nature take its course. It took two generations before the *Canticle* was fully crewed."

"I never heard that story before. So what're you getting at, Cha'ril? I'm still waiting on that question."

"Aignar, am I pretty?"

He fumbled with his tool, dropping his leg to the ground, and turned his helm to her in stunned silence.

She picked his leg up and put it back on his lap.

"If the answer is no and you are too polite to say so, I can—"

"Wait. What? We've crossed into this whole weird area and I'm a lot more confused now than when we started talking."

"You have a child. Clearly this ex of yours considered you acceptable for matrimony and procreation. Was it a combination of relative attractiveness and earning potential? Family arrangements? Purely a by-product of intoxication? I remember Roland and Masako after our night out in Australia."

"Yeah, those two were stupid for each other."

"I do not have a child. Having one while I am armor is not impossible. I was never one for dating, and now…" She touched the back of her helm, miming the plugs into her skull. "Naked augmentation is not attractive on a Dotari."

"I never…never thought of you that way," Aignar said. "What makes one human attracted to another is very personal."

"I see," she said, turning her attention back to his leg.

"But if I was a Dotari guy, I'd ask you out," he said. "I've seen you getting looks in the mess hall. Don't kid yourself—I bet they all think you're a ten."

"Ten what?"

"Out of ten. Do Dotari date like human teenagers? Is there someone you want me to talk to? Wow…here's a conversation I never thought I'd have in the Armor Corps."

"No. Never involve yourself in Dotari courtship. Not unless you want to provide both the dowry and witness to the consummation."

"Forget I asked."

"But thank you, Aignar. If I was a human female, I might try and get you drunk."

"No, that's not…thank you. Also, never say that to any human guy. Ever," Aignar said.

"Is there some sort of—"

"Oh look! Transports." Aignar pointed over the mountain ridge to several Destrier aircraft in the distance. "I need to get dressed. Hurry up with my leg."

****

Roland drifted in and out of sleep as his Mule rumbled through turbulence. His armor was in "storage" configuration, folded into a trunk shape the size of a small cargo container and bolt-locked onto the floor of the transport. Even though the space within his womb hadn't changed, he always felt cramped in the more compact configuration.

Aignar was in the same Mule, along with almost two dozen somber colonists.

"Roland, you asleep?" Aignar asked him over IR.

"Yes." Roland tensed his muscles, which

strained against the first actual effort they'd done in days.

"Good. Something's been bugging me about what Gideon said. Most of 3rd Squadron defected—went with the Ibarras, right?"

"That's what he said."

"I've been studying lance heraldry since I found out we were going to stay with Gideon and be Iron Dragoons. Historically, Dragoons were heavily armed infantry soldiers that rode into battle on horseback. Our heraldry comes from the American army unit that fought in the Iraq War in unarmored vehicles, oddly enough. So—"

"You're rambling. You only ramble when you're scared."

"I am not scared. I fight inside humanity's most perfect killing machine. I fear nothing…but I am concerned," Aignar said.

"You're 'concerned' over heraldry?"

"All the lances that went 'missing' with 3rd Squadron had their official files closed—pretty standard when there are battle losses, but not with

MIAs. General Laran and the top brass must want them forgotten, which I can understand."

"Rambling."

"The Templar keep their own records, tracking who's gone through the rites and stood vigil at Memorial Square. I was looking into 3rd Squadron's Templars…and they were Templar."

"There are Templar in every squadron and most every lance that's not Dotari," Roland said.

"No. They were *all* Templar. Every last one of them. It didn't hit me until I saw the cross on that sword they gave you."

Roland's jaw clenched tight. "Why?" he asked. "Every Templar we know is dedicated to Earth. How could any—"

"Not Earth, humanity," Aignar said. "Saint Kallen is the iron heart that never wavers. We will take our oaths to ideals, not politics. Maybe this is why Gideon is borderline hostile to us joining the order."

"Almost a third of Mars' armor is Templar," Roland said. "Do you think High Command thinks they might…follow 3rd Squadron to the Ibarras?"

"I always thought it was odd that Laran was promoted to general and Corps Commander over Colonel Martel. She's *not* Templar. He is."

"Damn the Ibarras," Roland said. "They caused this entire mess. Maybe we can end it all in this system before humanity splits into factions for good."

"You're not wrong," Aignar said, "but don't you wonder why those Templar went with them? What would make you leave the Corps, leave Mars…leave it all behind?"

"I don't know. I don't want to know. We've got enough real problems on Oricon. I don't need to add hypotheticals to my list." Roland shifted inside his womb. His armor rocked against the deck, startling a colonist sitting next to him.

"Yeah, sorry. I'll let you go back to sleep," Aignar said.

Roland shut off the IR link…but sleep never came.

CHAPTER 12

"From what little telemetry data we picked up," Strickland tapped his control screens and crescent-shaped Kesaht fighters maneuvered in the middle of the holo tank, "their void superiority craft are not as maneuverable as our Eagles, but they are a hair faster. While we don't know how many they lost fighting the Ibarrans, at the worst case, we're looking at no more than a thousand by the configuration of their capital ships."

Holograms of the fleet's strike carrier captains and their wing commanders stood around Lettow's tank. The admiral crossed his arms and looked at the *Falkland*'s captain, Hormond.

"We can get ninety birds in the void," Hormond said. "One on one, our pilots are the best out there, except for the Dotari. From what little we saw at the tail end of the Ibarra fight with them, the Kesaht fighter tactics are almost…amateur. We can handle any mission you give us, but we get swarmed with bogies and the situation will be in doubt."

"Understatements are not helpful," Lettow said. "What if they sent every fighter they have at once?"

"The crews know the old Xaros drills," Strickland said. "Each ship has spike shells and a volley of flechettes off the rail cannons would be effective. Haven't seen a fleet do a full on thresher since we taught the Naroosha a lesson."

"Have all ships run anti-fighter drills," Lettow said. "I'm concerned about the missiles we saw them using, their tracking software and warheads."

"The Ibarras know," Hormond said. "Something tells me they won't share if we ask nicely."

"It's in the Ibarras interest for us to bleed against the Kesaht," Lettow said. "We take a beating and we might not have the combat power to bring their fleet to heel."

"And I thought they might be redeemable," Strickland said.

In the holo tank, alert icons pulsed over every ship in the *Javelin* squadron. Lettow frowned and tapped the *Scimitar*, the squadron's lead ship. The ship's bridge had gone offline, but the rest of the systems were still functioning. The same failure was happening to all the artillery ships.

"Damn peculiar," Lettow said. He pulled down a menu on the *Scimitar* and opened a channel to the captain.

A vid link of Lieutenant Commander Wibben came up; the vid bobbed up and down as the man ran.

"Wibben. What's going on?" Lettow asked.

Wibben's eyes widened, startled as the admiral appeared inside his visor. "Complete power failure on the bridge, sir. Airlocks engaged just before most of my bridge crew could evacuate. Moving to secondary stations near engineering. We're working on a solution now, and trying to get Ensign Talson out of there."

"Sir," Strickland's eyes were wide, "just got updates from the rest of the artillery squadron. "They're all reporting the same failure…and that one crew member is locked inside the bridge. All of them."

"What the hell…" Lettow zoomed in on the afflicted ships. Then, the error codes vanished. Strickland looked at the admiral and shrugged.

The artillery squadron flashed amber as their weapons systems came online and the long vanes sticking out of their prow charged with energy.

"They're targeting one of the Kesaht battleships," Strickland said. Lines traced from the squadron to the massive Kesaht ship at the center of their fleet. The lines also passed through the cruisers *Zurich* and *Beijing*. Count down timers appeared next to the artillery ships.

"Order the cruisers to get out of the line of fire," Lettow said to Strickland. "Comms, raise the Kesaht and tell them there's some sort of malfunction."

"I…I can't, sir!" the lieutenant said. "The system just locked me out of the long range array."

"Wibben! Shut down your rail gun," Lettow said.

"Controls reverted back to the bridge," Wibben said. "Talson's the one doing this and he won't answer me."

"Get back onto your bridge and you shut him down," Lettow said through a clenched jaw.

"Cruisers are out of the line of fire," Strickland said.

"Comms?" Lettow asked.

"No joy, sir!"

He considered ordering the *Ardennes* to open fire on his own ships, but the command would barely be out of his mouth once the timer fell to zero.

"No sign the Kesaht have any idea what's

happening," Strickland said.

The artillery ships jerked back in sequence as their massive rail cannons fired shells the size of a small car down the twin vanes aimed at the heart of the alien ship. Even with the blistering speed of the shells, it took nearly thirty seconds for the rounds to close the distance.

Lettow forced himself to keep his eyes open, knowing that he was the commanding officer of the fleet that declared war on a new alien species, whether he gave the order or not.

A rail cannon shell lanced through a destroyer-sized vessel just before it struck the Kesaht battleship, a shield flared across the massive ship's prow. The shell careened off and struck the stern of an escort, sending it spinning out of formation.

"They have shields?" Lettow asked no one.

The next two hits delivered a one-two punch that sent a wave of static crackling along the port side. The last two hit simultaneously, stabbing through and ripping down the battleship's keel. It split in half like an axe through a log of firewood.

Debris bounced off the remaining Kesaht battleship, sending ripples down the ship's forward shields. To the battleship's stern, a spinning cannon tube hit the irregular hull plates and chiseled one away.

"But their shields are directional…" Lettow processed this new bit of information as he resigned himself to a fight he hadn't provoked, but the Kesaht would likely insist on fighting.

In the holo tank, the *Scimitar* went offline with a total power failure.

"Admiral," Wibben came up, his breathing coming quick and shallow, "my chief engineer tripped the emergency shut down sequence. I'll be back on my bridge soon as we get the doors open. Have to use the manual gears and it's taking time."

Lettow nodded and closed the channel. The other artillery ships kept pace with the rest of the fleet. None of their rail guns had recharged for a second volley.

"Kesaht fleet accelerating to attack speed,"

Strickland said.

"Comms?" Lettow asked.

"Systems are back on line but…they're not answering our hails," the lieutenant said.

"Orders, sir?" Strickland asked.

The Kesaht fleet reformed, their claw ships and battlecruisers settling in front of the remaining battleship.

"Ten minutes until we enter weapons range," Lettow said. "Ten minutes to stop this from getting worse. Keep our current readiness level. Do not launch fighters. No aggressive moves."

"They come swinging while our guard's down and—"

"We have time."

The holo tank pulsed red as sensor reports flooded Lettow's screens. He skimmed over the raw data and frowned.

"A lepton pulse from the Kesaht? Why would they…" Blood drained out of Lettow's face as the pieces clicked together.

New target icons appeared in the holo tank.

Around the outer edge of the Crucible, Kesaht battlecruisers emerged out of stealth. The ships accelerated forward, closing on the 14th fleet like a giant maw.

Then and there, Lettow knew more bloodshed was inevitable.

"They were there the whole time," Strickland said.

"It was a trap," Lettow said. "At least we moved out before they could trigger it." The 14th was outnumbered almost three to one, but the enemy was split into two parts. The new ships started flat footed and would take time to overtake his ships. When they joined the battle with the Kesaht ships hurtling straight for them, the scales would tip far out of Lettow's favor. He opened a channel to his captains.

"Hear this," Lettow said. "We have a fight on our hands. All ships will advance in formation at best speed. We've got the chance to defeat this enemy in detail and we will take it. Give them fire and fury. Any that survive will speak of this day with fear for the rest of their lives."

Alerts came through from the rest of the artillery ships; they'd secured their bridges after the lone sailor locked inside had opened the doors. That it happened on so many ships at the same time told Lettow the event was no coincidence.

"Strickland, we've got traitors on our ships," Lettow said. "We're going to root them out once this fight is over. Then we're going after the Ibarras to make them pay for this."

****

"Torp launch," Strickland said.

Icons emerged from the Kesaht fleet guarding the battleship and streaked toward Lettow's ships. He watched them trace down their projected courses; this first launch sent two torpedoes toward each of his forward cruisers.

"They're feeling us out," Lettow said. "Engage counter missiles and point defense at max range. Let's see what they've got."

"Aye aye."

A dozen small missiles shot from square cargo boxes bolted to outside of the cruiser's hulls and closed on the incoming torpedoes…which moved at an almost languid speed in comparison.

The smaller Kesaht destroyers, their forward hulls bent into the shape of a clawed hand gripping at a target, sprinted ahead of the rest of their fleet.

What's your game, Gor'thig? Lettow thought.

The counter missiles closed…and the torpedoes sprang forward, afterburners blazing. The leading counter missiles tried to swerve into an intercept course, more whiffed through the torpedoes' trail. The back field of missiles exploded in the torpedoes' paths, showering them with metal fragments and small magnetic balls full of denethrite.

A handful of the torpedoes made it through the phalanx of counter missiles. All but one fell to point defense turrets; the final scoured a hit against the *Beijing* and exploded with a flash. The cruiser emerged, trailing hull fragments and a thin line of ice.

Seconds passed painfully as Lettow waited for an update.

"*Beijing* reports moderate damage to three decks," Strickland said. "Weapons and propulsion unaffected. Some casualties, no number yet."

"Launch bombers, minimal fighter escort. Have them target the incoming destroyers. Bombers will execute the hook on my command. Long range rail cannons on our cruisers and frigates focus fire on these ships." Lettow said and marked three battle cruisers above the alien battleships. "Have the artillery ships open sustained fire on the battleship."

"Aye aye." Strickland sent the commands off in seconds. "That flagship's sure to have shields. You think our artillery can get another golden BB through the shields?"

"I doubt it, but if I was the enemy commander I'd be afraid of just that after my sister ship got ripped in half. I want to know if Gor'thig will use his other ships as shields. Xaros had no centralized leadership. The Ruhaald would do anything to protect their queens. I don't know about these Kesaht."

Rail cannons across the 14th's leading cruisers fired as quick lines closed on the alien ships. There was a flurry of rockets from point defense turrets, but the effort was too little, too late. Rail shells pounded the targeted cruisers. One exploded into a ball of fire and expanding debris. The second broke in half, the still-burning engines corkscrewing back toward Oricon. The third stopped dead in its tracks, flashes of small explosions bursting through the hull.

"They're running under atmosphere," Lettow said. "If anything gets through the hull, they'll have to deal with fires…if blast waves don't kill the crew."

"Best we not interrupt them while they're making that mistake," Strickland said. "They've got plenty more cruisers for us to blow up…not including the ones coming up from behind."

The admiral checked on the distance

between his command and the closing ships. Still almost forty minutes until they reached weapon range, which was an eternity during a battle.

"Spread out the rail targets," Lettow said. "See if a single hit is enough to take their ships out of the fight. No need to let them soak up rounds."

"Admiral, the Kesaht are hailing us," the comms lieutenant said. "It's coming from the ship near Oricon."

Another volley of torpedoes launched from the alien ships.

"Keep up the pressure," Lettow said to Strickland. "I'll keep this brief."

He double tapped a screen and the Sanheel officer appeared in the holo tank.

"Treacherous animals," Gor'thig snarled.

"There are rogue elements within my fleet responsible for the attack on your ship," Lettow said. "I can share logs and prove that—"

"We know your history. What you're capable of," Gor'thig said. "I should have crushed you when I had the chance."

"You mean those ships you had hiding around the Crucible? So if I hadn't weighed anchor, I'd be the one sputtering about 'treachery.' We can avoid further bloodshed." He glanced at the holo tank. The incoming torpedoes arced off their initial course and converged toward the *Javelin* squadron.

"No," Gor'thig said, baring his teeth, "this will be my day—when the Kesaht Hegemony met the great evil and struck the first blow. I will carve the name of your broken ship into the Ascendant Steps myself. My ship will not destroy all of your infection on the moon. I would have your home world know that their reckoning is coming for them."

"If you bombard civilians, there will never—" Lettow's lip twitched as the channel cut off.

"What the hell was he talking about?' Strickland asked.

"Damned if I know." The admiral checked the time estimate until the battleship near Oricon would have line of sight to Auburn City. The location of the city on the far side of the planet was likely the only thing saving the city from the battleship's guns.

"Sprint!"

The Kesaht torpedoes made a sharp course correction and angled toward the cruiser *Ottawa*. The ship threw up a flurry of counter-missiles and fire from her point defense turrets, but the overwhelming mass of incoming targets overwhelmed the cruiser's defenses. A torpedo hit the upper hull and exploded, ripping the top of the ship open. Another torpedo slipped through the gap and detonated within the ship. The *Ottawa* shattered into a thousand directions.

"Adjust line spacing to half," Lettow said, watching a red X icon pulse over where the *Ottawa* used to be. "Overlap point defense envelopes, make it harder for them to overwhelm a single target."

The *Ottawa* had eight hundred souls aboard. He doubted any survived.

He turned his attention to the claw ships closing on his destroyer screen. The Condor bombers had just entered weapon range and tracks from their torpedoes appeared in the holo tank. The torpedoes, much smaller than the Kesaht weapons, jinked from side to side, guided by a bombardier on the firing Condor.

The claw ships offered an anemic defense, barely more than a few laser bolts from a single turret at the "palm" of the ships. Torpedoes hit home, erasing the Kesaht ships from space. The reaming ships pressed forward, unfazed by the losses. Several dozen of the ships still remained.

The *Ardennes* rumbled as her rail cannons joined the fight. The holo tank filled with crisscrossing rail shots and torpedoes. His ships took damage, but none as catastrophic as the *Ottawa*.

The Kesaht suffered, losing a dozen ships in the first thirty seconds of the exchange.

"Maintain fire on—"

The deck lurched beneath his feet, tossing him against Strickland. The holo field flickered.

"Took a hit to the upper decks," Strickland

said. "Power nodes to the port rail batteries are off line."

"What the hell was that?" Lettow jabbed a fingertip against his screens, working to recalibrate the holo tank. The image finally resolved…and several of his ships were blinking amber with damage.

Half the claw ships blinked as the sensors read a massive power surge. Light built at each of the fingertips. Laser beams fired into a single point, then a massive beam lanced down and into the Terran fleet. Every claw ship that attacked exploded or burnt away as the lasers overloaded.

The *Ardennes* shook again.

The cruiser *Sao Paolo* went offline, canting to one side as her engines misfired from a direct hit. The *Edinburgh* went dead in space, and debris trickled from a pierce through the top and bottom of her hull.

"Destroyers, break off and engage the remaining claw ships," Lettow ordered. He did a double take at the holo field as fighters swarmed out of the Kesaht ships and made straight for the *Ardennes*.

CHAPTER 13

Dinkins slapped a hand over a thigh pocket and his face knit with confusion. He wiggled against the straps securing him to the Mule's bench and pulled out a data slate in a bulky case. He did a double take at the screen, then unbuckled himself.

"Sir! Return to your seat!" a crewman shouted from the fore of the cargo bay.

Dinkins knocked on Roland's armor.

"Hello? Are you awake in there? I think I've found them—the children!" Dinkins knocked again.

"Sir! Please—"

"Kiss my ass!" Dinkins held the data slate over Roland's optics.

"What am I looking at?" Roland asked.

"The bio trackers came online. We must be in range of the city's towers. The request went through and-and—just look!" Dinkins tapped on the slate again. "All fifteen children just pinged. See?"

"They're one hundred fifty yards above ground level and moving at almost two hundred miles an hour," Roland said. "They must be in a Kesaht aircraft."

"Then how do we get them—" The Mule bucked, sending Dinkins face-first into Roland's side, then nosed downward, losing altitude rapidly.

"You should sit down," Roland said. He tapped into the Mule's turret feeds. Auburn City was on the horizon; columns of smoke rose around squat apartment high-rises and the sprawling supply parks surrounding the city.

The foreman struggled back into his seat and buckled himself down.

"Couple Kesaht fighters tried to jump us," Gideon sent over the lance channel. "Eagles made swift work of them. I'm trying to raise Captain

Sobieski, but what channels are open are chaos. The Kesaht just launched an assault on the city and the primary comms towers were the first thing they hit."

"Sir, Dinkins found the missing children. On an enemy craft moving to the northwest," Roland said.

"Looks like that's where they're going." Cha'ril sent an image of a massive Kesaht ship flying toward the moon, just beyond the atmosphere, its hull partially obscured by high, thin clouds.

"Can the Eagles catch the shuttle with the children?" Roland asked. "Force it down without—" The Mule's upper turret opened fire, earning shouts of fear and surprise from the colonists.

"We've got our own problems here," Gideon said. "Stand by…I think I've got Sobieski."

"Fight to save the city or go after the children," Aignar said. "I know which choice the townies will make. It's their kids."

"Battlefield math," Roland said. "Gideon

and Sobieski will send us where we'll do the most good, save the most lives. Emotions won't be a factor for them."

"Sometimes I'm glad I'm just a warrant, not an officer with gold or silver bars. I don't have to 'what if' too many decisions at the bottom of the totem pole," Aignar said.

"Hey!" Dinkins waved the data slate in the air. "They're breaking for orbit. Do something!"

"That's a tracking device, right?" Roland popped a data port open on his right forearm, which was folded up next to his helmet. "Give it to me."

"But you said—" Aignar began.

"You never know." Roland cut him off as Dinkins unstrapped himself and stumbled against Roland as the Mule banked hard.

"You snap your neck and see if I care!" the crewman yelled at Dinkins.

Dinkins stuffed the tracker into Roland's forearm and slapped the metal twice.

"Find my boys," Dinkins said. "Ask the Saint to find my boys for me. For my wife."

"If I can reach them, I'll bring them back to you. I swear it," Roland said.

"Here's the mission," Gideon said, breaking into the channel. Archive pictures of a massive supply depot to the city's south came up on Roland's HUD. "Kesaht broke through the walls and have artillery somewhere in this area. They're pounding the city center and Sobieski wants us to take it out. The Mules will do a combat cargo drop to get us close to the fight."

"Sir," Cha'ril chimed in, "we aren't palletized nor are we fitted with arresting parachutes."

"This plan lacks finesse," Gideon said.

"And once that's accomplished?" Roland asked. "What about the children?"

"We will reevaluate once Sobieski can regain control of the battlefield. Anytime the defenders try to maneuver, they get hammered. Prep for landing," Gideon said.

The Mule's ramp opened and air howled through the cargo bay. A crewman jogged past

Roland and unsnapped the pair of bolts at his feet. The crewman shouted at the passengers to press against the wall, promising they would lose any body part that touched the armor on its way out. The crewman went to Roland's head and placed his hands on the last two bolts securing him to the floor. The outskirts of Auburn passed beneath the ramp and the Mule dipped low and banked to a highway. The thunder of artillery and *brrrt* of Eagle cannons joined the howling wind.

"Hey in there," the crewman shouted over the wind, "pilot wants you to know he'll cut his airspeed as much as he can...just don't get angry if you get a little banged up."

"I'll take it out on the enemy. Fair enough?" Roland asked.

"Here we go. Three...two—" The Mule lurched up as the blast wave from a near miss knocked the ship off course. The crewman pulled Roland's bolts up and he slid down the carbo bay.

Aignar's crewman pulled up one bolt by accident, and the corner of his armor slammed into the side of the Mule, almost crushing a colonist's legs. They got the last bolt up and Aignar slid down at an angle.

Roland fell free from the Mule and found himself ten yards over a highway with idle cargo trucks along his intended landing path. He hit the road so hard it made his earlier torpedo breaking maneuver feel like a tap on the shoulder.

His armor bounced up and plowed through a drone-driven hauler. He burst through the cab and landed on top of a smaller truck, splitting it down the middle, then juddered across asphalt and slowed to a stop.

Roland unfolded from his cargo configuration and got to his feet. Ammunition lines connected to his gauss cannons and a line of electricity danced up his rail cannon vanes as his armor became fully operational.

"Aignar?"

There was a crash behind him. Aignar rolled down the highway, spinning like a barrel and wrecking every vehicle in the way. He crashed into a cargo container on a truck bed and came to a stop halfway through the other side. Metal bars poured out of the container and struck the ground, ringing like a giant's wind chime.

"Aignar!" Roland ran to his friend.

The other armor's arms unfolded, knocking away the loose bars, and Aignar fell through the other side just as Roland arrived. As Aignar stood up, he stumbled against another truck, mashing the cab and shattering the windshield.

"You all right?" Roland asked.

"Sure. Fine." Aignar took a step forward, then veered to one side before he bumped against the cargo container that stopped him. "Just…a little dizzy. Which way do we go?"

The thunder of artillery pulsed from the west.

"Toward the sound of gunfire," Roland said. He jumped over the guardrails and fell two stories. He landed in the midst of stacked cargo containers. Frozen robots stood in place at half-open doors and in the gaps between rows, many still carrying items.

Aignar dropped in behind Roland and bumped his shoulder against an open container door, ripping a tear across it.

"You sure you're all right?"

"It's like sobering up. Got to give it a minute while trying not to barf in your roommate's shoes." Aignar said and then ran past Roland.

"You said you were never going to mention that again." Roland cycled gauss shells into his cannons.

"And you believed me. How adorable," Aignar said.

"This is Gideon, Dragoons respond," came over the IR.

"Roland. We made landing and are en route to target location."

Gideon and Cha'ril's location came up on his HUD. They were a dozen rows away and moving fast.

"Speed up," Gideon said. *"We hit them at the same time."*

Roland and Aignar ran faster, passing a

section of stacked containers riddled by bullets and leaking brown nutrient paste. An Eagle fighter roared overhead, trailing smoke and fire. Roland kept running as he heard it crash into the cargo yard. Yellow tracer fire stitched across the sky just beyond the edge of the supply yard.

"Air defense emplacements," Aignar said. He jumped up and grabbed the side of a container, then climbed up the stack.

"Gideon wants us to—"

"You want us to go get those kids? We're not going to sprout wings and fly into orbit. I'll catch up." Aignar got his head and shoulders over the top of the stack and brought his gauss cannons to bear.

Roland cleared the edge of the cargo yard. The Kesaht artillery were massive tracked vehicles. Dozens of vehicles with wide-barreled cannons angled high and crewed by Rakka blasted off another volley. Rakka in powered exo suits carried fresh rounds from ammunition haulers lined up behind the artillery pieces.

Tanks formed a loose perimeter around the artillery. Snub-nose turrets with belt-fed chain guns slewed toward Roland.

"Let's see what you've got." Roland aimed his gauss cannon where the tank's turret met the lower hull and fired. The rounds tore through the turret and the tank exploded, hurling the top section into the air.

Roland jumped to one side as another Kesaht tank fired. The shell struck the ground and peppered Roland's armor with shrapnel and pulverized asphalt. Roland put two rounds down the enemy tank's cannon and it vanished into a burst of flame and smoke.

"Their ammo storage is poorly armored," Cha'ril said. "Shoot the rear third of the turrets."

Roland swung his cannon arm toward a tank aiming at the other two Dragoons and fired a single shot. The magnetically accelerated round struck the turret with a spark and the tank exploded a split second later.

The closest artillery piece's treads squealed

to life. It spun in place to face the oncoming armor and the massive cannon lowered, coming to a stop level with Roland.

Roland let loose with his gauss weapon, but the shells bounced off blue-white shields that flashed with each impact. Rakka crew looked over the top of the artillery piece, pointing at Roland. Even running at full speed, the Rakka would have a hard time missing him with a weapon that size.

He slid to a stop and raised his left foot. The diamond-tipped anchor spike popped out of his heel and he rammed it into the ground, bringing his rail cannon up and over his shoulder.

"You don't have time for that!" Cha'ril shouted. "Move!"

The Rakka ducked behind the cannon aimed right at him.

"I need ten more seconds." Roland charged the accelerators at the base of the vanes and fed a lance bolt into the chamber.

The sky split with a crack. Roland winced inside his armor, thinking the alien artillery had beat him to the draw. He opened his eyes and saw a smoking crater where the Kesaht weapon had been a second ago. A shadow passed over him and the forward half of the cannon tube sailed through the air, the base peeled open. The fragment landed behind Roland and bounced into the cargo stacks.

The crash of metal on metal sounded across the battlefield. Then again. And again. A line of cargo stacks fell over, knocking the next row over and then the next. The cargo stacks fell like dominos.

"Aignar?" Roland asked.

"What are you waiting for?" Gideon called out.

Roland turned his attention back to the Kesaht artillery park, where another cannon had lurched forward and was coming to bear on the armor. Roland aimed his primed and ready rail cannon at the artillery, then shifted his aim to the line of ammunition haulers.

He braced himself against the ground and fired. Firing a rail cannon in atmosphere was akin to being in the middle of a sonic boom. The recoil from the shot and overpressure rocked Roland back; only his anchor kept him from going airborne like he'd been slapped by a giant.

He felt impacts against his armor and fell to one knee. He looked up at the Kesaht artillery position…and found nothing but flames and mangled metal. His rail cannon shot had obliterated the ammunition carriers and the subsequent explosions had taken care of the rest of the Kesaht vehicles.

"Roland. Status," Gideon sent.

"I'm fine." Roland drew his anchor back into the housing within his leg. Through the smoke billowing around the destruction, a Rakka in powered armor stumbled out. Its skin was black and blistered, and blood oozed from its ears and mouth. It looked at Roland and managed a grunt, then picked up a jagged hunk of metal and walked toward him, limping on a broken leg.

The Rakka thumped the improvised club against its chest.

Roland blew its head off with a gauss shot, then turned back to the still-falling dominoes in the supply yard. At the top of the nearest fallen stack, a cargo container went tumbling down the slope, breaking against the ground and spilling thousands of small boxes. Aignar sat atop the pile, his anchor stuck through a hunk of loose metal that had once been a cargo container.

"You're welcome." Aignar said, sheathing his anchor and made his way down the pile.

"Quick thinking from both of you," Gideon said as he and Cha'ril ran over, the barrels of their forearm cannons glowing red and smoking.

The sound of collapsing stacks echoed through the supply park.

"You think the colonists will be angry about the mess?" Cha'ril asked.

"Captain Sobieski said destroy the artillery," Aignar said. "He didn't say anything about being neat and tidy about it."

Gideon looked up at the Kesaht battleship over the horizon.

"I've got Sobieski on the line," the lieutenant said. "Roland…go to container Z-A-1138. Bring me what's inside. The rest of you go to X-X-62211. Bring four units. Hurry."

Roland looked out across the seemingly never-ending stacks of cargo.

"What am I looking—"

"You'll know it when you see it. Move!" Gideon looked away from them and toward the city center.

Roland ran to a robot porter at the edge of the stacks and ran data lines into the robot's access ports. The robot came online and rolled away, attempting to carry out its last command. Roland picked it up and re-tasked it to open container Z-A-1138.

"Please don't be in that mess," Roland muttered as he looked at the widening pile of fallen containers.

The robot's wheels spun furiously and he set it down. It zipped away, heading to the outer edge of the chaos. Roland followed and turned a corner to find it stopped next to a jumble of containers.

"Balls." Roland looked over the serial numbers etched onto the sides, he saw 1138 and climbed up the pile and ripped open the side of the container. Inside were cube frames with bright yellow boxes bolted inside. He pulled one out and saw explosive warning symbols on the yellow boxes.

"Denethrite," Roland said. Mining charges meant to fell mountains. The explosives were somewhat shock-sensitive, but; a hard-enough hit could detonate them with unfortunate results for anyone too close.

Reaching inside, he found a box of the detonators and gently climbed off the pile of containers. While the denethrite was packaged and designed not to explode under anything but the kinetic strike of a missile, he wasn't one to tempt fate.

Roland met up with the rest of his lance, who'd returned with four cases the size of a normal clothes trunk.

"You know you knocked over enough explosives to crack this moon's shell," Roland said to Aignar.

"Oh." Aignar said, crossing his arms, "guess I should've stopped to take a full accounting of everything in here before I used my rail cannon to save your ass. You're still welcome, by the way."

Gideon looked away from the city center and over the retrieved items.

"Good," the lieutenant said. "Roland, you have the tracker?"

Roland tapped his forearm.

"Sobieski's given us the go for a rescue mission. Two Mules are en route. We haven't seen the Kesaht use any anti-grav systems. The captain thinks they aren't at that tech level yet, which means we may have a way to sneak up on their flagship."

"And if they do have the technology and are scanning for anti-grav fields?" Cha'ril asked.

"Then the operation won't end well for us," Gideon said.

CHAPTER 14

Roland's Mule broke through the anvil-top of a thunderstorm and wobbled as it passed through the high winds of a jet stream. Roland, mag-locked to the top of the Mule to one side of the upper turret, kept his focus on the two pilots, one of whom looked up at either Roland or Aignar, locked to the other side of the turret, every time the Mule veered with the air currents.

Between the armor, the gunner manning the turret held up a data slate and took a selfie with Roland, then spun the turret and took another picture with Aignar.

"We're not that aerodynamic, are we?"

Aignar asked.

"I never thought I'd prefer being strapped down in the cargo bay," Roland said.

"Don't know about you, but I'm about done with cargo anything." Aignar raised his helm and looked back to the moon. "I see the other Mules and our escorts. No contrails. We're on anti-grav thrusters now."

Ahead, the Kesaht battleship continued its course, skirting the moon on the way to the Crucible gate. The flash of the 13th Fleet's rail cannons and Kesaht plasma bolts crisscrossed space near the Crucible. The gas giant loomed beyond the battleship, like a baleful eye watching the conflict.

"Fleet said they tracked the shuttle with the kids to that battleship." Roland accessed the tracker in his forearm, checking that it was fully charged and integrated into his system.

"Damn big ship for the four of us to go poking around," Aignar said.

"The tracker will narrow down where to look on the ship," Roland said. "Just hope we can fit in their hallways."

"Those Sanheel are our size, shouldn't be a problem…Why do you think they want the kids so badly? The Kesaht pulled a battleship off the line to make the pickup. I'm no ship driver, but that doesn't strike me as the best tactical decision."

"Doesn't matter. They're counting on us. Their parents are counting on us." Roland touched the sword hilt still locked to his leg.

"What're you going to do with that when we get back to Mars?" Aignar asked.

"You think the big brass will let me keep it?"

"You think they're going to let you walk around with concrete proof that armor's gone renegade? Unless you want to trade it for a nice hand receipt from the military police, we need to find a sailor unburdened by scruples to get it to Mars for us."

"I doubt Gideon would buy that I dropped it somewhere and don't know where it went. He used to be enlisted like you. Knows all the same tactics that straight commissioned officers don't know yet."

"And Cha'ril would narc on us in a heartbeat," Aignar said.

"She's been acting strange lately," Roland said. "Ever since her leave to Dotari was cancelled, she's been…"

"Prickly? I noticed. Maybe she's got a boyfriend back home."

"She won't even say why her leave was cancelled. Not for performance or behavior issues, that's for sure."

"Some Dotari political thing?" Aignar asked. "They seem pretty stable on their home world, but up until a few days ago, I thought everything was hunky-dory for Earth. Now…where is the Ibarra fleet? You have any idea where those legionnaires went?"

"One fight at a time, right?"

"The recruiter never said the Armor Corps would be boring."

The turret gunner tapped against his cupola,

then toward the rear of the Mule.

A hand reached over the edge and slapped against the hull, locking a magnetic hand grip onto the metal. A crewman crawled over the edge and snapped another mag lock attached to his knee onto the Mule. He lugged a case up over the edge, then crawled toward Roland.

"You look nervous," Aignar said.

"I hate…EVA," the man said. He was sweating profusely, soaking a cloth band around his forehead with impressive speed. "First, I had to put together an anti-grav impeller while on ascent. Now I get to carry this damn heavy thing to you while that dickhead Gurski films me and laughs his ass off."

In the turret, the gunner had his data slate out and was indeed laughing, the sound hidden behind the vacuum of space.

"Because he *knows* I hate EVA," the crewman said, creeping forward, "and he *knows* it's supposed to be my turn in the turret." He stopped and passed the case to Roland. The armor removed an anti-gravity generator with a giant handle welded to the frame.

The crewman pressed his middle finger to the turret, which made Gurski laugh even harder.

"Where's mine?" Aignar asked.

"Yes, sir." The crewman crawled back to the edge of the Mule. "On its way."

Gurski rotated the turret around for a new selfie with his struggling crewmate.

"Aignar," Roland said.

Aignar tapped a finger against the turret twice. The gunner's head snapped to one side and he went pale as Aignar's helm stared at him. Aignar opened his hand as wide as the gunner's head, then pinched the fingertips together. Gurski pocketed his data slate. The armor jerked a thumb toward the approaching battleship, and Gurski nodded so fast Roland thought he'd break his neck. Then the turret turned toward the fore of the Mule and the gunner focused on his duties.

"Armor, this is your pilot," came from the Mule. "We are one hundred seconds from your release point. What's your status?"

"Your EVA just delivered the second impeller," Roland said. "He needs to get inside or the blowback might send him Dutchman."

"Love my job." The crewman muttered, crawling away a little faster. "Love my job. Love my job."

"It'll take us at least ten minutes before we can reorient for a pickup," the pilot said. "We'll wait for your signal after that. Good hunting."

Roland activated the impeller and felt a slight tug as the anti-grav waves formed.

"Release in ten…" the pilot said. Roland lessened the mag lock between his forearm and the anchor point on the Mule and braced his feet against the hull. "Three…two…one…go!"

Roland stood up to a crouch and activated the impeller. It accelerated, dragging him along with it. He looked back and saw Aignar catching up to him and the Mule turning back to Oricon.

"Really wish they'd had some proper jetpacks in that supply yard," Aignar said. "At least the navy had breach charges for us. I'm not sure why Gideon wanted Cha'ril to carry the denethrite, and not me."

"I can't imagine why," Roland said flatly.

The battleship grew nearer and Roland angled the impeller toward the sharp edge along the side of the hull. He zoomed in on open missile tubes, point defense emplacements, and fighter bays with crescent-shaped fighters held fast on their launch rails. If the Kesaht saw the armor on approach, there wasn't any sign of a response.

Gideon and Cha'ril waited at the rendezvous point, both lying with their backs and feet against the hull. Roland swung the impeller away from the ship and pulsed the anti-grav, slowing him to the point where he set down on the hull with hardly a sound. Aignar landed a few meters away.

Roland felt the thrum of the battleship's engines through the hull, the irregular hull plates making him feel like he was on a cliff looking up at a peak of a shattered mountain.

"Cha'ril, set the charge," Gideon said.

"Roland, let's hope that tracker's still working."

"On it." Roland accessed the tracker and brought up the control menu on his HUD. He readied the PING command and looked over the edge to the other half of the battleship. A glass pyramid at the center of the slope stuck out like a sore thumb.

"If I had to guess…" Roland activated the ping and waited as the tracker cycled through radio frequencies. A blob of light came up on his HUD, six dots just below and to port from a cannon battery.

"I would have guessed wrong," Roland said. "There's only six returns. Still nine children unaccounted for."

"Scan again before we breach," Gideon said. "Cha'ril, you set?"

"Denethrite locked down and detonator set," she said. "I gave you all the trigger codes before we left the ground."

"Think this will be enough to destroy the ship?" Aignar asked.

"Terrans used half as much denethrite in the warheads that took out Toth cruisers and Xaros constructs," she said. "This is overkill. Not that I'm complaining. Explosions are meant to make a statement."

"Move out." Gideon said and then flipped over the edge, using his impeller to skim along the battleship's surface. Roland followed, scanning for any sign they'd been detected while he maneuvered around the uneven hull.

Gideon came to a stop in a small defilade next to the battery. He locked his impeller to the hull and pressed his palm against the dull red metal. Tiny spurts of atmosphere escaped around his fingertips as probes burrowed into the ship.

The Dragoons locked their impellers to their backs.

"They're running under atmo…stupid," Gideon said. "Damn amateur hour if they get into a void fight with their hull full of oxygen that can fuel fires and a medium for blast waves to blow the ship apart. No wonder they haven't overrun the 13th."

"Yet," Cha'ril said. "Quantity has a quality all its own."

Roland zoomed in on the glass pyramid, where several Sanheel worked in different tiers. One wore a golden sash over its chest and had red-colored lanterns fixed to the armor over where the leg joined the rest of the alien's body.

"The captain, I presume," he said. "Doesn't look like they're in any state of alert."

"Found a corridor." Gideon pointed to the edge of the defilade. "No burn cord, the explosion would put the hostages at risk. Use a breach-and-seal kit."

"Roger, sir." Roland opened a small case on his lower back and removed a compact metal frame. He snapped it open with a flick of his wrist and stretched it out to a square just large enough for his shoulders to fit through. He pressed the frame against the hull for a moment, and a small drill spike bored into the dull red surface. Cutting lasers ran up and down the four sides, sawing into the hull. Air hissed out of the cuts, then a square breach fell into the ship.

Roland jumped into the ship, minding the thin metal lines still gripping the outer hull section pressed to the deck. The Kesaht corridor was wide, with slightly raised walkways on the sides and two sets of cargo rails running along the floor. He pinged the tracker again, and five signals returned to him, all in the same location.

Air rushed past him, escaping through the breach. The *whoop* of emergency sirens grew fainter as the air thinned to almost nothing.

"Clear," Aignar said as he jumped down. The breach kit lifted the hull section back up and sealed the gaps along the edges with foam that hardened instantly.

"I've got them," Roland said. He ran down the corridor and thanked the Saint that the Kesaht built their ships to accommodate the larger Sanheel. He had barely enough room to spread his arms while on the *Scipio*, and getting around the much larger *Ardennes* in his combat configuration was a chore.

Air pressure returned, forced through vents along the ceiling. Roland heard the clunk of a door opening around a corner. He took the corner at speed and bore down on a half-dozen Rakka carrying welding tools and wearing helmeted void suits.

The Rakka were stunned at the sudden appearance of the towering armor charging right for them. Roland thought that he would have likely reacted the same way if he was told to go repair a hull breach and was greeted by an alien mechanical monstrosity.

He used their brief shock to close the distance, then crush five of them against the bulkhead with a single kick. One ducked away from the blow and tried to scamper away. Roland slapped a hand over its head and crushed its skull. He picked up one of the Rakka welding tools, a metal pole with a torch at the end, and jammed it into the doorframe where the engineer team had come from. He wedged another torch into the other side.

"Should buy us some time," he said to his

lance.

The whoop of the warning siren changed to a high-pitched double chirp. The passageway's lights changed from white to red, then back and forth, over and over again.

"I don't know Sanheel shipboard operations," Aignar said, "but let's assume they know we're here."

"Keep moving," Gideon said.

Roland heard grunts and barked commands farther down the connecting hallway. Rakka rushed around a corner and fired on Roland, the bang of their rifles echoing off the walls. Bullets bounced off Roland's chest and the side of his helmet. He deployed his shield from his left arm and ducked behind it to protect the sensitive optics in the helmet that the Rakka were aiming for. He brought his rotary cannon up and over the edge of his shield and let off a two-second burst that shredded the oncoming Rakka.

He backed up and turned to follow the rest of the lance. The aliens weren't returning fire—his attack had been effective.

At a T-intersection at the end of the corridor, Cha'ril and Aignar had their shields out, firing their gauss cannons around the corners. Gideon had one hand pressed to the ceiling, his probes scouting the surrounding structures.

A Sanheel rifle shell struck the deck and ripped through the utility lines beneath the plating. A fountain of water spurt into the air and was quickly burnt into steam by another Sanheel shot.

There was a *thwack* as an alien shell hit home. Cha'ril pulled back from her spot against the wall, a spike a foot and a half long embedded in her shield. She swept her cannon arm down the shield and broke the spike, leaving the metal tip still embedded, then stuck her twin-gauss cannons around the corner and fired off a double shot, earning a scream of pain from down the hallway.

"We can get to the children's location," Gideon said, "but both options are full of hostiles."

Roland activated the tracker, and three dots appeared, all on just the other side of the wall. A realization sent a chill through his heart.

"They're killing them." Roland ran past Gideon through the line of fire, and smashed a fist against the bulkhead separating him from the chamber with the kidnapped children. His first blow tore through the wall, and he gripped the breach with both hands and pulled. The tear widened with a screech of metal. Inside were dark boxes the shape of coffins and glass pods along the walls filled with deep-blue fluid.

A Sanheel spike ripped the anti-grav impeller off Roland's back. He kicked at the bottom of the gap he'd opened and created an opening big enough for him to get through. He stepped past one of the pods and snapped his gauss cannons to one side.

Two children sat on a raised dais at the end of the chamber, both hunched forward, their hands cuffed. The third sat on the lap of a humanoid alien that had thin limbs that would have brought it to eight feet tall if standing, and almond-shaped eyes that wrapped around its temples. Glittering cables ran from the base of its skull to a heavy collar that drooped over its shoulders and down to the middle of its chest. It stroked the hair of the child on its lap, who winced every time the alien touched it.

One of the coffins was half-open; inside was a girl maybe eight years old. Her eyes were closed, and hair floating around her face like she was underwater. Light glowed around her from inside the box.

"My, my," the alien said, "the stories of your ferocity are true. Amazing that such aggression can evolve from something as innocent as this." It wrapped a long finger around the boy's neck.

From the hallways, the sound of gunfire died away.

Roland advanced into the chamber, cannons leveled at the alien's face.

"You want to see fury?" Roland asked. "Hurt one more child and you'll get to see it firsthand. I'll turn your corpse into a testimony of just how angry we can get."

"I've not hurt anyone," it said. "I am

Tomenakai, of the Ixio, of the great Kesaht unity that will welcome humanity, if only you submit."

"Then what did you do to her?" Roland glanced at the girl in the box.

"Stasis," Tomenakai said. "These broodlings are so afraid. It will make the journey home so much easier for them. I told them of the gift we were going to give them…once we work past a few biological issues."

"They're going to put computers in our brains," said the boy sitting at Tomenakai's feet. "Take away our thoughts. Make us do what they want."

"Submission for peace," the alien said, "the end of conflict, the end of want. Sanctuary from all fear and desire. You will realize how noble our offer is, especially in light of humanity's crimes. Your genocide. If base savages like you can be redeemed, the whole galaxy can live in the paradise the Kesaht can provide."

"I am taking the children with me." Roland stepped closer to the dais. "That will happen.

Killing you is optional."

Tomenakai gripped the child's throat a bit tighter and opened his mouth to hiss at Roland. Fangs extended from its mouth. Roland lowered his gauss cannons and brought his hand just over the hilt mag-locked to his leg.

"But I need them," the alien said. "Human adults have failed to accept our unity. The false minds in weed bodies are too aberrant. The solution lies with your young. If they can be brought into unity and absolved of your race's crimes, then you all can be redeemed. If not, then all of humanity must be purged."

Shadows emerged in the pods. Humans floated into view, all with their skulls exposed, cybernetic parts fixed to their brain matter. All had their mouths open in silent screams.

The children began whimpering.

"Failure is the price of science," Tomenakai said. "If I examine the union between your brain and your armor, the solution might—"

Roland snatched the hilt off his thigh and

lunged at the Ixio, activating the sword and snapping out the blade. The tip stabbed through the alien's neck and burst out the back. Roland twisted the sword and popped the alien's head clean off. He chopped the blade down and severed the hand gripping the little boy's neck.

The boy jumped off the alien's lap and ran to the boy on the dais, who unwrapped the hand from the other's neck and threw it away. The two boys hugged each other, the younger almost bawling into the other's chest.

There was no blood from the alien's body; only clear fluid seeped out of the cuts.

"This will be remembered," came from Tomenakai's head where it lay on the dais. "The final act of humanity's damnation!"

Roland put a foot against the alien's head.

"Our salvation will never come from you." Roland said and then stabbed his anchor spike through the alien's head, splattering it across the dais.

The snap of gauss cannons resumed.

"Roland!" Gideon shouted. "We can't hold them off forever!"

Roland went to the three children and bent down.

"What're your names?" he asked.

"I'm Chris Dinkins," the older of the two boys said. "This is my brother Ben. That's Suzy Oldman."

Roland opened the case on his lower back and brought out shrink-wrapped vac suits.

"You know how to put these on?" he asked.

"I want to go home! I want my mommy!" Suzy screamed.

Roland looked at the delicate spacesuits held in his giant fingers. Armor was designed for brute force, not something so intricate as putting a child into an oversized vac suit.

"I know how to work the boxes," Chris said. "I saw the big one doing it right before they put us inside on Oricon. It's easy."

"Show me," Roland said. Chris went to the girl inside the half-open coffin and closed it. He touched two fingers to a shiny panel, but nothing happened.

"I know." The boy said and picked up the Ixio's hand, touching the panel with it. The box hissed and sealed shut. Roland did a scan and found it to be airtight and shielded enough to handle the void.

"I need you all to get inside." Roland pointed to empty coffins.

"No!" Ben howled.

"Listen to me." Roland tapped his chest. "I am inside something just like that right now. I get scared every single time I put on my armor. Right now, I need you all to be braver, stronger than I am. Find the iron in your hearts and get inside so we can leave."

"You'll take us home?" Suzy asked.

"The first person you see when you wake up will be your parents. I swear," Roland said.

A Sanheel spike ripped through the wall and cracked the top of a tank. Blue liquid gushed out and spread across the floor.

"Come on, Ben." Chris led his brother to an empty stasis pod. Ben stepped inside and pressed his fists to his eyes. He froze a split second later. Chris sealed the pod with the dead alien's hand.

Suzy stood in front of a pod, her hands clutched to her chest.

"I don't know, Chris," she said. "The last time I—"

Roland bumped his knuckles against her and pushed her into the pod. Chris slammed it shut.

"Thanks," Chris said. "She's always like that." He passed the alien's hand to Roland and backed into the last stasis pod.

"You remind me of that one armor in the movie everyone's seen about the Dotari," Chris said.

"Don't have time for this, little man," Roland said as he gently gripped the Ixion's wrist between two massive fingertips.

"I think his name was Elias."

Roland shut the coffin and sealed the boy inside.

One of the chamber's side doors opened and Rakka came flooding through. Roland activated his flamethrower and swept the flames over the intruders. The room filled with black smoke and high-pitched screams from the alien foot soldiers. Roland looked up at the smoke billowing across the roof.

"I think we're near the hull," he said. "Burn cord."

He took a canister out of the box on his lower back and attached the bright red cord to the ceiling, forming a rough hexagon. When he touched the cord with his flamethrower's pilot light, the entire length ignited. Molten metal dripped down as the cord burned through the ceiling. Gray smoke spat through the gap as the cord went higher and higher, and then the smoke stopped and the ceiling burst up like a cork. The void sucked all the smoke out of the hole in seconds, along with the rest of the chamber's air, and the other Dragoons came into the chamber, their shields pitted and chipped.

The smoke stopped, then the ceiling burst up

like a cork. The void sucked all the smoke out of the hole in seconds along with the rest of the chamber's air. The rest of the Dragoons came into the chamber, their shields pitted and chipped.

"That breach activated their emergency bulkheads," Gideon said. "Cut them off from us. Doubt it'll stay that way long."

"Time to leave, yeah?" Aignar asked.

Roland jumped up and climbed out of the still-smoldering hole cut through the hull. Aignar came up after him and took his anti-grav impeller off his back.

"Roland, where's your—never mind, I'll do it." Data wires snaked out of his wrist and into the impeller.

"Catch." Cha'ril tossed a stasis pod up the breach and into Roland's waiting hands. He passed the box with the child inside to Aignar.

"Jolly Greens, this is Dragoon-3 requesting immediate evac," Roland broadcasted. He caught another box and handed it off to Aignar, repeating the transmission again and again while shuttling the coffins out of the Kesaht ship.

"Nothing heard, sir," Roland said to Gideon.

"I think I see them." Aignar sent a target icon to Roland, a point well behind the battleship. Roland zoomed in. A hull section of the battleship floated in the void, turning end over end. On one half was the denethrite bomb.

"Not them," Roland said. "But the Kesaht did find our parting gift." Roland caught the last of children.

Aignar had all the coffins pressed into a rough sphere against his impeller wedge, which pulled the coffins against it like a magnet.

"You can reverse the anti-grav waveform," Aignar said. "Make it pull instead of push. Course it does strain the system awful hard. It'll burn out in less than an hour. Times like this I wish we had rope in our kits."

Cha'ril and Gideon crawled out of the ship as Roland looked across the hull to Oricon, which seemed farther away than ever.

"I think…I think I'm out of good ideas,"

Roland said.

"We need to signal for pickup." Gideon put himself between the stasis pods and the distant denethrite bomb. "Shield wall."

Roland unfolded his shield and came shoulder to shoulder with Gideon and Cha'ril. Gideon touched the side of his helm, and Roland ducked behind his shield.

A blinding flash of light broke across the battleship, like a new sun had been born and burned away in an instant. A surge of heat flooded his shield and spiked into his arm, and he felt pain in his arm within the womb, a psychosomatic reaction to the damage his armor suffered.

"That should get their attention," Gideon said.

"Contact." Cha'ril pointed over the edge of the battleship where crescent-shaped fighters arced over the hull.

"Think they'll fire and risk hitting their own ship?" Aignar asked. Yellow bolts of energy spat out of the fighters and shot overhead. Bolts struck the side of the cannon battery, smashing the armor into fragments.

"Dumb question." Aignar fired gauss shells at the oncoming fighters, breaking the wingtip off one and sending it spinning into the alien ship next to it. The two exploded into fireballs against the hull.

"They can see us from the bridge." Cha'ril planted her anchor and brought her rail cannons to bear on the crystalline pyramid, then loaded a shell into the chamber.

Roland took a fighter's energy bolt to the shield and skidded back across the hull, stopping only after Gideon grabbed him by the shoulder. Roland pumped shots after the fighter as it flew overhead. One round connected and snapped the alien ship in half. The two sides tumbling into the void like loose scythes.

"Cha'ril, I want you to miss," Gideon said.

"To what?" Cha'ril did a double take at the lieutenant.

"You heard me." Gideon fired on four more

fighters coming over the prow of the battleship.

Cha'ril's rail cannon flashed, the effect of being near a rail cannon firing much more subdued in the void than on the moon's surface. The remains of a cannon battery toward the far edge of the ship tumbled away into the void.

"I missed the bridge," she said.

In the pyramid, the Sanheel crew looked up from their workstations. The red-clad captain pushed aside the other centaur he'd grabbed as an impromptu shield.

"Reload," Gideon said.

Cha'ril held up another shell, then slowly and deliberately put it into the chamber.

"I can't fire again for two minutes," she said. "The capacitors need to charge."

"We know that, but they don't," Gideon said.

The Sanheel captain waved his arms and the fighters broke off their attack and flew to the other side of the battleship.

"I am off standing with a Mexican, correct?"

Cha'ril asked.

"Almost," Roland said. "Just keep looking like you want an excuse to blow them all to hell."

"I don't need an excuse. I need permission."

"Dragoons, this is Jolly Green 6," came over the radio. "You've got a swarm of bogies on the ventral side. My escorts don't have the combat power to break through and make extraction."

"This is Gideon," the lieutenant said. "We've reached a tentative agreement with the Kesaht. Bring the Mules in for pickup and hold fire. Can you relay a tight-beam message to Captain Sobieski?"

"Negative on tight beam, wide only. Enemy likely monitoring."

"Tell him a trained Uhlan with a lance could spear a loaf of bread out of a man's hand. I expect he can do better," Gideon said.

Cha'ril looked at Roland, who shrugged.

Two Mules approached, their bottom turrets turning from side to side.

"Cha'ril, you and I stay here until the

children are clear with Roland and Aignar," Gideon said. "Roland, the instant your Mule gets clear, you send a wide-band message to Sobieski. Tell him '*ogien.*'"

"Yes, sir." Roland pulled a coffin off the impeller and waited for a Mule to arrive. It stopped a few yards above the hull and spun around. He pushed the stasis pod into the Mule, where the transport's internal gravity gripped it and sent it to the deck. The crew pushed the coffins to the back of the cargo bay and frantically strapped them down while Roland and Aignar got the rest of the children inside.

"Lock up and go," Gideon said, waving the second Mule closer.

As the Mule lifted its nose, Roland jumped off the battleship and powered up the mag lock on his forearm. His arm smacked against the hull, and Gurski, in the turret pod, waved to him. Roland mimed crushing his head.

Aignar locked on and the Mule fired its afterburners to leap away from the battleship.

Eagles fell in beside the transport.

"Captain Sobieski," Roland sent on every channel his armor could access, "Gideon sends 'ogien.'"

On the battleship, Cha'ril's rail cannon flashed and the ship's bridge shattered into a million fragments.

"What the hell are they doing?" Aignar asked. Roland watched as Cha'ril and Gideon loaded up onto the other Mule. Beneath the battleship, a swarm of fighters broke loose and flew toward the upper half of the ship.

A red line zipped up from the moon and slammed into the Kesaht ship. Fire billowed from the impact and hunks of hull plating shot out, destroying a dozen crescent-shaped fighters.

"That was from a rail cannon," Roland said.

Four more rail shells struck in quick succession, ripping through the flight decks. The battleship canted to one side, exposing her ruined hull. Two more shells streaked up from Oricon and punched clean through the ship. Fire spattered from the damage as the ship's atmosphere bled out.

The battleship exploded, shooting the prow forward and spreading the rest of the hull across the sky like chaff pulled from wheat.

"Gideon? Cha'ril?" Roland asked over the broad spectrum.

He switched his sensors to IR, searching for the heat plume from their Mule's afterburners, but the remains of the Kesaht ship clouded his sensors.

"No," Aignar said. "No, no, no…"

"Dragoons, this is Gideon."

Roland thumped a fist against his chest to thank the Saint.

"Took a hit on our way out," Gideon said. *"Crew is unharmed, but our Mule is disabled. Send a search-and-rescue bird at your earliest convenience. By that I mean before we burn up in the atmosphere or we find another piece of space junk with our name on it."*

"On it, sir," Roland said, "and sir, you're right not to trust the Kesaht to let us get away."

"If an enemy wants honor or mercy, they

need to show some first. Get the kids back to their parents. Well done, Dragoons."

****

Captain Sobieski knelt on the cracked pavement of a supply yard, his rail cannons smoking hot. He watched as the last of the Kesaht battleship's burning wreckage faded away, then he raised his anchor back into his leg and stood up.

He turned to the armor still kneeling in the remains of the alien artillery the Iron Dragoons had destroyed. Smoke and smoldering metal formed a hellscape around the armor, and damaged residential towers creating a battered skyline beyond the yard.

"Steel on steel." Sobieski struck a fist against his chest. "Good shooting."

The armor returned the salute and replaced their rail cannons on their backs.

"Orders, sir?" asked Lieutenant de Saxe of the Chasseurs.

"Get to the spaceport. The admiral will need us soon," Sobieski said.

CHAPTER 15

The 14th was in the middle of a slug fest. The outer edge of Lettow's frigates had meshed with the Kesaht's screen and were trading cannon and rail blows at what amounted to knife fighting range for void war ships.

The aliens' crescent-shaped fighters died in droves to the fighters off the *Gettysburg* and *Falklands* and his ships' point defense turrets, but there were so many of them. Gor'thig's fighters had managed to inflict some damage, and their mere presence was a distraction, like trying to fight with gnats in your eyes and ears.

"Hormond, where's my hook?" Lettow

asked the *Falkland's* commander.

"Got twelve bombers coming up on the flagship." Hormond appeared in the holo screen. "Can put fifteen torps in space. Spent most of our ordnance on those damn claw ships. Give them three minutes and keep the enemy looking straight ahead."

In the holo field, a small group of bombers and a few fighter escorts closed on the rear of the Kesaht battleship. The engines created a sensor baffle that should mask the bombers' approach until they launched their torpedoes.

A pipe in the bulkhead on the back of the bridge burst, punching a dent toward the holo tank. Steam shot through a crack in the blister.

The communications lieutenant screamed and gripped her helmet. She tried to twist it off, but a sailor pinned her arms to her sides in a hug before she could spill her air into the near vacuum on the bridge.

She shook her head from side to side.

"There was a transmission off Oricon!" she

shouted. "Cut through everything!"

Lettow reached into the holo tank and pulled the moon to the fore. The battleship that was in distant orbit was in ruin, the hull perforated by multiple rail cannon strikes.

"Sir, the flagship." Strickland moved the holo image back to the battle. The last remaining Kesaht battleship accelerated forward, the engines burning bright.

"Raven three!" Hormond said, announcing that the bombers had loosed their torpedoes.

The massive Kesaht ship burned forward, on a course straight to the Crucible gate. A course that took them perilously close to the *Ardennes*.

"None of the other ships are trying to break through…" Lettow said.

Behind the battleship, cruisers swerved into the torpedoes' line of fire, taking the hits meant for the flagship.

"Guns, ready a full volley when the ship passes," Lettow said. "Helm, adjust course to give us a clear shot."

The Kesaht ship barreled forward, its shields flaring as rail cannon shots hammered away at the prow.

"Come on, you bastard." Lettow gripped the holo tank and said a quick prayer to Saint Kallen.

The fleeing battleship came parallel with the *Ardennes* and her rail cannons fired. Lettow felt the ship shudder with each shot. Shells hit the shields covering the front half of the ship, the after effects fading out just ahead of the Kesaht's engines. A shell smashed into the flank and a gout of fire exploded from the ship. Two more rounds hit home, and a still burning engine broke off the ship. When the *Ardennes* struck again, every hit bounced off shields.

"They're rotating their shields," Lettow said. "Keep up the fire…" He touched a cruiser on the opposite side of the Kesaht ship. "*Hamburg*, you should have a clear shot from your angle. Hit them!"

The cruiser's turrets slewed toward its new target. The rail cannons flashed and scored direct hits on the battleship's hangars. The ship trailed fire from its belly…but it didn't stop moving.

"Their fighters." Strickland pulled up a gun camera feed where a turret blasted apart the crescent fighters. The enemy fighters had shut down, traveling on their last vector.

The battlecruisers that had been hidden around the Crucible changed course, maneuvering behind the Kesaht flag ship.

"Hamburg, disengage," Lettow sent. Fire from the alien ships he'd been fighting had slackened. Their ships meandered away from each other. The 14th did not relent, destroying the ships one by one.

"Pursue?" Strickland asked.

"No." Lettow shook his head. "We break formation to chase them down and we'll be vulnerable to what we're already fighting. They want to run…let them."

It took another hour to mop up the last of the Kesaht ships. On long range scanners, Lettow watched the battleship flee through the Crucible gate along with the last of the alien fleet. He breathed a sigh of relief when the wormhole collapsed and the Crucible remained in one piece.

"What happened?" Strickland asked. "That ship around Oricon wasn't going to make a difference to the fight. If they got those ambush ships into the fight…I doubt we'd be talking right now."

"Armor," Lettow said. "Armor happened. They did something to send the Kesaht running with their tail between their legs."

He touched a screen and a smattering of life pods appeared in the holo field.

"We can piece together what happened later. Get search and rescue in the void, we need to save our people," he looked over his surviving ships, all of which sported damage, "and lick our wounds."

CHAPTER 16

At the spaceport, Roland pressed Tomenakai's fingers against the last stasis box. The lid hissed open and the light around Ben faded away. The little boy pulled his fists away from his eyes and blinked at his brother and his parents, the Dinkins.

"Mommy! Daddy!" Ben fell into his parents' arms and the four hugged each other.

Tim Dinkins looked up at Roland and mouthed a thank-you. Roland nodded and turned to a group of anxious-looking scientists. One held up an empty specimen jar. Roland dropped the severed hand inside and the scientists practically giggled as they looked it over.

"Anything else you can tell about the specimen?" asked a woman in a lab coat.

"It didn't die when I cut its head off," Roland said.

She looked up from her data slate. "I'm sorry, did you say 'cut off'?"

"Yes. With my sword," Roland said.

The woman swallowed hard and backed up a step.

"It stopped talking after I crushed its skull." Roland lifted his foot and extended his anchor tip out of his heel. "There might be some of it on there."

She covered her mouth and ran off.

"What?" Roland kept his foot up as another scientist scraped gray matter off his spike.

"You get her number?" Aignar asked as he walked over.

"You find out what our next mission is?"

"Squat and hold until transport arrives. The captain's working the mission details now," Aignar said.

"I'm low on ammo and I need to recharge or hot swap my batteries." Roland put his foot down as the scientist left with the sample.

"Cap said we'll get that on the transport. We move soon as they hit dirt," Aignar said. "I didn't get all the details, but I heard 'Ibarra' a couple times."

Roland looked over at Sobieski, standing in the middle of an ad-hoc communications node bristling with directional antennae.

"The captain's Templar," Roland said. "Should we tell him about the sword? This Morrigan person?"

"You go over Gideon's head and he's liable to crush yours with good reason," Aignar said. "If the Corps had suspicions about the Templar, even aspirants like us, they'll only get worse after this. You give even an impression we're loyal to anything but the chain of command and you'll look guilty."

"If Gideon goes straight to General Laran

with this—"

"He'd jump both Sobieski and Colonel Martel. Gideon's a hard-ass. He may not like the Templar, but he's as straight as they come."

Roland touched the hilt on his leg.

"Politics. Hated it in school. Didn't think I'd ever deal with it in the Armor Corps."

"It's more for the big brass. Line grunts like us get to focus on killing bad people and breaking their nice things. But…look at that." Aignar said, pointing to the edge of the flight line, where the rescued children were looked over by doctors and run through decontamination spray boxes. "Families. Families made whole because you refused to fail them. Imagine the hell those parents would have gone through if those alien shitheads got away with those kids. War is shit. Death. Destruction." He cocked his head toward the chaos of the wrecked supply yard. "We're lucky to get through it with scars and nightmares. But you, kiddo, you were a goddamn hero today. When those bad days come, and they'll come, don't ever forget this moment—the smiles on those kids' faces."

"You were there too," Roland said.

"The Saint was with us. Maybe we can go to her shrine when we get back to Mars."

Roland thought back to the small cave where Kallen was interred within her armor and he tasted her "tears" again.

"We should…I would like to see her again."

Over the spaceport, four corvettes descended from orbit.

"Dragoons," Gideon came over the IR.

"Always ready, sir," Roland said.

"The Scipio *picked us up in orbit. Report to her soon as she lands. We are needed."*

CHAPTER 17

The maintenance rig around Roland's armor almost felt like home. A team from the *Scipio's* crew worked to ream and recharge his armor, operating with none of the finesse of the Iron Dragoons' dedicated team of Brazilian armor tenders. Master Chief Henrique had cross-trained this group of navy ratings. Roland could almost hear the chief's colorful Portuguese euphemisms as the sailors struggled to load a fresh case of gauss shells into Roland's ammo stores.

The rest of his lance stood in their bays, recharging off the ship's batteries. Gideon was off their network, online with Captain Sobieski and the other commanders.

"But what did that big ugly mean about 'humanity's sins,'?" Aignar asked. "This is our first contact with them. It's not going great, but it sounds like he's talking about something else."

"The Ibarras have interacted with them in the past," Cha'ril said. "Perhaps they committed some diplomatic slight or killed a Kesaht leader. Such things have happened before."

"The Ixio had human bodies in its lab. The Ibarras knew how to fight them," Roland said. "I'd think the Ibarras wrote a check that Earth gets to cash, but he accused us all of xenocide. I don't know when, where, or why the Ibarras would exterminate an alien species. Seems a bit far-fetched."

"Humanity destroyed the Xaros," Cha'ril said. "Annihilated their Dyson sphere and sent their drones into the nearest star."

"That was the old Alliance," Aignar said. "Us, the Dotari, Ruhaald, Qa'Resh—before they up and vanished—don't know why these Kesaht would single us out. I don't see any of the Xaros in these Kesaht. The Xaros wiped out every intelligent species they encountered. That Ixio was talking about some grand union through brain implants. Doesn't fit."

"So the xenocide he's talking about probably isn't the Xaros…then who?" Roland asked.

Aignar turned his helm to Gideon.

"The lieutenant got hurt pretty bad by the Toth," Aignar said. "Still totes around some of their claws. But he never mentions them. No one ever talks about the Toth anymore. They showed up around Earth, demanded proccie tech and that we hand over a significant portion of our population. Sure, 8th Fleet—may the Saint preserve them—kicked their ass and sent them packing, but High Command's doesn't even list them as a threat species. We don't even train to fight Toth targets."

"The *Breitenfeld* carried out a punitive mission against Toth leadership soon after the incursion," Cha'ril said. "They killed the senior

Toth overlord and rescued a number of prisoners from the planet…Nibiru, I think it was. The Toth were said to have descended into civil war after that. Then the Qa'Resh destroyed all the jump engines before they vanished. The Toth are very likely stuck in their home systems with no means for faster-than-light travel."

"The tech for making Crucible gates was disseminated across the old Alliance…if they had it, we would have encountered them again," Roland said.

"The Toth were *not* part of the Alliance," Cha'ril said. "Therefore, they did not receive the Crucible technology. The answer is evident. No species would willingly contact a race of slavers and murderers. We are well aware of what the Toth do to prisoners."

"There were some crazy stories from the end of the war," Aignar said. "Especially from the *Breitenfeld*'s crew. Weird energy beings. Giant machines feeding off suns."

"Didn't the *Breitenfeld's* crew get

preferential colony assignments after the war? I don't think any of them are on Earth. Who was there at the end?" Roland asked. "Colonel Hale went on that deep-space colony mission. Admiral Valdar is on some secret assignment…"

"Miss Bailey was badly injured at the last battle," Cha'ril said. "She says she doesn't remember much of what happened."

"The Ibarras were there," Aignar said. "I bet they know everything."

"We might have a chance to ask them," Gideon said. "Our mission plan is coming through. I'll share it in a moment."

"Sir, what happened to the Toth after the Ember War?" Roland asked.

"This is relevant, how?" Gideon asked.

"Something the Ixion said to me while he was ranting about 'false minds and weed bodies'—"

"Stop," Gideon said. "Are you sure he said that? Those exact words?"

"I'm sure," Roland said. "Do they mean something?"

"It's…nothing, just jogged some old memories." Gideon's armor brushed fingertips across the helm, tracing his facial scars. "The Toth are a low-threat priority. We train for fights we're likely to have. Not theoreticals."

"But what happened to them?" Aignar asked. "It's like they vanished."

"I don't know and I don't care," Gideon said. "We have enough enemies without picking fights with old ones. You three ready for our real-world mission or do you want to keep playing 'what if?'"

The lance remained silent for a moment.

Gideon activated a holo projector in the ceiling of the *Scipio*'s bay, the gas giant Oricon Prime and her moons forming over the hellhole. An icon for a small flotilla of corvettes and destroyers popped up between the colony moon and the pale-brown planet. A dashed line for the flotilla's course ran over the planet's north pole.

"Just what the Ibarras want with this system was a mystery until a few hours ago," Gideon said.

"When the Ibarras first arrived in system, they had this exchange with the governor."

Two pictures came up in the holo, one of a recorded video of Governor Paletress, a woman in her late forties with short bobbed hair, the other a still silhouette of a person's head and shoulders.

"Where is it?" A wave form matching the words appeared beneath the silhouette. "Your survey records from six days ago show exactly where it is. Stop toying with me."

"Admiral…Faben, was it?" Paletress sighed heavily. "As I've told you, we don't process the raw data. We; we simply compile and send it on to Earth for analysis. Three hours before you arrived, High Command restricted the data with a clearance level I've never seen, and one neither you nor I have the codes to unlock. Your demands are most irregular and I don't see how—"

"You still have the raw data," Faben said. "Send it to me."

"Admiral," the governor said, putting a hand to her face, "the data is encrypted. There's no way you can access it without the key cipher. My programmers say that even with a quantum dot—"

"Send it. To. Me."

"I will not." The governor squared her shoulders. "This system is under the colonial administration. It is not under military jurisdiction, and even if it was under my control to release it to you, I wouldn't give it to you, even on the off chance you might choke on it."

The governor looked offscreen.

"Another Crucible wormhole." She narrowed her eyes and one corner of her mouth pulled back in a smile. "Let's hope it's the alert fleet I requested from Earth come to teach you some decorum." The governor's eyes narrowed, then she went pale. "What are those ships? Who are they? Jackson, run a full scan and—"

The two frames blinked off.

"You can piece together the story up until now," Gideon said. "The Kesaht landed troops on Oricon and the Ibarras fought a running battle for three days until our fleet arrived. Fleet intelligence went looking through the data the Ibarras asked for and found it had been accessed not long after we arrived."

"The Ibarras put spies on the moon," Roland said. "They must have landed them along with their legionnaires."

"Not just the moon," Gideon said. "An infiltrator's been discovered on the fleet. Intelligence thinks there's a significant risk of there being more spies, or sleeper agents, within the fleet's proccie crew."

"But the true born aren't suspect," Roland said. "That's why the admiral's sent the armor on this mission? We can be trusted."

"That wasn't put out in the mission order," Gideon said, "but I agree with your assessment."

Aignar looked down at the hilt on Roland's leg.

"The fleet's computer techs found that the data the Ibarran commander demanded was no longer encrypted at all. The storage units were a bit older…and built by the Ibarra Corporation," Gideon said.

"They built themselves a back door into the system," Cha'ril said.

"The data was from a probe doing deep radar scans of the gas giant," Gideon said. The holo zoomed to the north pole, an ivory white storm several times the size of Earth. A blinking black square appeared near the center.

"What is it?" Roland asked.

"An anomaly is all we know right now," Gideon said. "From what the probe could detect, it out-masses the Crucible gates and there's probably more of it beneath the storm layer."

"It must be an artifact of a dead species," Aignar said. "Nothing like that has ever been found in a gas giant. The gravity, and…this was buried in a report for bean counters on Earth to look at? I thought the Path Finder Corps would jump all over this."

"The probe's software classified it as an error," Gideon said. "How the Ibarras learned about it before the data scrubbers on Earth begs a number of questions."

"More spies," Roland muttered.

"Soon after the Ibarrans accessed the data, their fleet changed course for Oricon Prime." Gideon zoomed in closer on the anomaly. A grainy black dome appeared in the snow-white storm.

"We don't have as far to go and are faster. Captain Tagawa is certain we'll beat the Ibarras to the finish line. Our mission is to secure the artifact. Prevent the Ibarras from leaving with anything of value."

"How would the Ibarras get away with it?" Aignar asked. "Damn thing's bigger than the Crucible gate."

"Such structures have been encountered before," Gideon said. A holo of a sphere with circular gaps in the surface appeared. Beneath the outer layer spun a similar inner shell, beneath that was another, and another. "Qa'Resh primogenitor technology."

"That's what the Vishrakath were after on Barada," Roland said. "They risked a full-scale war for it."

"That was a fragment. This…is considerably more," Gideon said.

"Turn it off," Cha'ril said. "It makes my head hurt."

The spinning object faded away.

"Admiral Lettow will move the entire fleet to secure the area once the Crucible is repaired and reinforcements from Earth arrive," Gideon said. "The Ibarras don't have the ships to stand up to our line, but he's not going to risk leaving the gate vulnerable and them locking us into the system again. The corvettes will insert us into the relic. Then we hold tight until the fleet arrives."

"And if we encounter the Ibarras?" Roland asked.

"Our orders remain. They surrender or they will be destroyed."

****

The *Scipio* rocked as it descended through

the polar storm. Roland had his feet locked to the deck, looking down through the ship's hellhole and into what looked like a blizzard raging just beneath the ship. The rest of the Dragoons formed a circle with him around the hole.

"Think we should ask Captain Tagawa how she's doing on the bridge?" Aignar asked. "I feel like we're in a Mule flying through a hurricane."

"I think she was dead serious about ripping your head off and defecating down your neck if you bothered her again," Cha'ril said.

"*Scipio*'s a good ship," Gideon said. "Trust her and her crew."

"Easy to trust when you're just along for the ride," Aignar said. "Not like you have any other options."

The ship wobbled from side to side. A supply crate broke loose from its moorings and went skidding across the deck at Roland. He slapped a hand down and stopped it dead in its tracks.

Roland looked up, then shifted his weight

from foot to foot. The turbulence was gone.

"Landing zone in sight," Gideon said.

Through the hellhole, an azure plain emerged from the storm. Thin fractals appeared and disappeared just beneath the surface.

"Whoa…" Aignar said.

"Each time I see one of our starships, or an orbital archology," Cha'ril said, "I think that our species have come so far, accomplished so much. Then this reminds us all that we are nothing but children…playing with our toys on the grand stage of history."

The *Scipio* slowed and came to a stop a few dozen yards over the surface.

"Tagawa here. Anti-gravs are encountering some sort of interference. I can't risk going any lower. You good for a little drop?" the captain asked.

"Drop is no issue. Recovery is," Gideon said.

"We can run winch lines. Better than the catch wires on Nimbus," she said.

"You've got a loose cannon down here." Roland slapped his hand against the supply crate.

"We'll have it secured before we scoot back to the fleet," she said. *"Be prepped for at least thirty-six hours before we return."*

"We'll stay busy." Gideon said and dropped through the hellhole.

Roland jumped down. Oricon Prime's gravity exerted slightly less pull than Earth's and he landed with a hollow bell toll as his feet struck the azure metal. Roland moved away from his landing spot and readied his gauss cannons.

In the skies above, corvettes dropped armor across the surface. The vistas were immense, the horizon of the gigantic structure far more than the three miles Roland was used to on Earth. The storm of ivory-colored gas raged over the artifact, but Roland felt nothing against his armor.

"Nitrogen," Gideon said. "Atmosphere is nothing but pure nitrogen. Half the pressure of Earth standard."

"I would say that's impossible, considering

this gas giant is mostly hydrogen and helium, but here we are on some ancient civilization's…what is it? Science station?" Roland asked. Cha'ril and Aignar dropped in behind him.

"We'll find out." Gideon looked up at the *Scipio*. "Tagawa, can you read me?"

"For once," she said. *"We've got tight-band coms back to the fleet from here. Destroyer* Kearney *will drop a relay buoy in geostationary orbit. You need us, we'll come running. Good luck down there.* Scipio, *out."*

"I don't see an entrance." Aignar thumped his heel against the surface. "Something tells me breach kits might not work."

"Sixty-five square miles of surface area," Gideon said. "Company commander wants us to do a grid search. Call out anything unusual."

"This whole place is unusual," Aignar muttered.

The Dragoons spread out into a line and started walking. Roland scanned back and forth over the glinting metal.

"Sir, did anyone manage to get into that other Qa'Resh facility?" Roland asked. "The one with the spinning layers."

"There's no definitive yes or no on that," Gideon said. "But there is a large number of classified files about that operation. If the *Breitenfeld* showed up and couldn't get past the front door, I suspect there wouldn't be as much to classify."

"The *Breitenfeld* again," Aignar said. "What didn't that ship do during the war?"

"It had the only jump drives in the Earth fleet," Cha'ril said. "That a strategic asset was put toward strategic goals isn't a surprise."

"It wasn't the only jump drive," Roland said. "Eighth Fleet had one, used it to slow the Xaros hive moon coming in from Barnard's Star. My father was on that fleet."

"Who wants to bet there was someone named Ibarra on the away team that went into the other Qa'Resh…thing?" Aignar asked.

"I wish we knew what they're looking for

here." Roland half-turned around and gazed up at the white skies. "Bet the Union could use whatever…where did that come from?"

Roland aimed his gauss cannons at a black circle several yards wide on the ground just behind them.

"That wasn't there a second ago," Aignar said. "I walked over it. We all walked over it."

The circle shimmered with surface tension, like the top of a glass of water one drop away from overflowing.

"Other lances are reporting the same thing," Gideon said.

"Roland," Aignar said as he punched his friend on the shoulder, "go rub your face in it."

"Piss off," Roland said. "Remember when you asked me to look in that crevice on Nimbus? I ended up with some sort of octopus thing on my neck doing…you know what it was doing."

"I believe it was copulating with your neck servos," Cha'ril said. "I still have several pictures if you're unsure what happened."

Gideon stomped a heel against the ground.

"Roland, you are the junior Dragoon," the lieutenant said. "Examine it."

"Sir." Roland said as he knelt next to the circle and snaked a camera wire out of his wrist. It moved through the black surface like it wasn't even there. Beneath was a long, evenly lit tunnel that sloped downward at a slight curve. The dimensions of the tunnel gave him pause, as the diameter appeared nearly double the width of the black circle.

"Lead's inside, plenty of room for us." Roland drew his camera line back in with a snap.

Gideon took a thin metal cone off his back and set the base against the edge of the circle. It locked against the surface, then unfurled into a satellite dish.

"Let's go." The lieutenant slipped into the dark portal. No sound escaped as his feet struck the tunnel walls.

Cha'ril got to the edge and hesitated.

"What's wrong?" Roland asked.

"Nothing. Nothing is wrong," she said, her voice strained. The Dotari put a hand next to the edge and kicked her feet up and into the portal. Roland went after her. His sabatons slid against the tunnel and he had to put a hand to the wall to slow to a stop. He looked back to the portal and saw a perfectly smooth black circle, almost perpendicular to the tunnel. Roland looked back down the tunnel, then back to the portal. The portal's angle felt…wrong.

"No walk path," Aignar said as he slipped through. "No residue on the walls. Guess we're not coming through a smoke stack or sewer line."

"We still have comms with the surface." Gideon raised an arm and swung it forward, the old hand-and-arm signal for "follow me."

While the tunnel still had a nitrogen atmosphere, Roland noted that his footfalls made no sound at all when they struck the tunnel walls. They descended for several minutes, the tunnel twisting down like a spring coil.

Their path leveled out and opened into a

dome that stretched for miles. In the center, sheets of gold and white glass the size of the *Ardennes'* hull plates spun slowly, their shapes changing from two-dimensional flame motifs to fractals dancing within fractals and star fields that shifted moment by moment.

"I think I'm going to be sick." Cha'ril looked away from the object.

"What the hell is that?" Aignar asked. "The way they're moving around each other, it's impossible."

"By my pace count, we've gone a little more than a few kilometers." Roland pointed to the ceiling. "That is ten kilometers high."

"Captain Sobieski warned that we may experience some non-Newtonian physics in here," Gideon said.

"Great." Aignar said, shaking his helm. "Space magic."

"Not magic," Cha'ril said. "Just a use of space and time we cannot explain."

"That is exactly how you define magic,"

Aignar said.

"Is that what we're looking for?" Roland pointed at the slow-moving wall sections in the center of the dome.

"I think it's…art," Gideon said. "Visitors arrive at the surface, descend through the tunnels, and see this."

"It is a mistake to put our own cultural patterns over an alien civilization so…alien," Cha'ril said.

"Let's just call it art until we figure out for sure if it's a Qa'Resh privy or not," Aignar said.

"Look." Roland zoomed in on white dunes around the base of the moving sculpture, the dark dot of a portal on each one.

Gideon walked toward the dunes, his stride long and purposeful. As they neared the dunes, Roland felt the ground shift slightly against his feet. He found himself standing in sand. He looked back and the once-solid floor he'd been on was now white sand.

"That's…odd," Roland said. He leaned to

one side to look at a pattern in the sand behind Cha'ril, and she shoved him out of the way.

"Move!" she hissed.

Roland walked to the pattern and sent a picture to his lance.

"Treads." Gideon stopped. "Armor treads."

"One of the other lances must have made it down here first," Roland said. "They would have left a mark for which portal they went through. That's protocol—right, Cha'ril?"

Cha'ril stood next to a portal, her helm angled toward the ground.

Roland pinged her systems and found her external optics were shut off.

"Cha'ril? What's wrong?" Roland asked.

"I am having difficulty…Dotari…we…" Her optics came back online. "We do not handle spatial irregularities well. Our eyesight is keen, designed to see and process information better than humans. When I look around, it's like my eyes are on fire. The angles are wrong. They're wrong!"

Roland looked at Aignar, who shrugged.

Gideon put a hand over her helm optics.

"Power down all external inputs but audio," the lieutenant said. "You're dangerously close to redlining, are you aware of that?"

"Just give me a minute," she said. "My system needs to adjust."

"Your neural load is far too high," Gideon said. "Your brain is trying too hard to make sense of information it can't."

"I am armor," she said. "I am fury, not some bundle of nerves. I will not fail this mission. I will not!" She tried to push Gideon's hand away, but he grabbed her by the back of the head. A panel on her helm slid open and access wires in Gideon's hand connected to her armor.

"If you redline, you will fail," he said, "and we would be less without you."

Cha'ril grabbed at Gideon's hands. There was a snap and Cha'ril's armor went rigid.

"I locked her in and set her armor to follow mode." Gideon stepped back and Cha'ril's arms fell to her sides. "The Dotari are usually resistant to any neural overloads...but this is a curveball. The only armor that's ever been in a place like this was human and they never had any problems. I'm taking her back to the surface. The *Scipio* hasn't gone far. They may be able to double back and extract her."

"One of us should take her," Roland said. "You've got—"

"Either of you ever walked someone back from the redline? I've trained you all since selection. Don't tell me you've picked up that skill while I wasn't looking. She—and this mission—are my responsibility," Gideon said. "You two keep searching. Follow search protocols. If I don't catch up to you in the next eight hours, return to the surface."

"But Cha'ril—"

"Where did I stutter while giving orders?" Gideon snapped. "What wasn't crystal clear?"

"We've got it, sir," Aignar said.

Gideon ran back to the tunnel. Cha'ril's armor followed, mimicking his stride perfectly.

"She'll be all right," Aignar said. "Good

thing the lieutenant knew how to recognize a near redline."

"I hate to think how he learned." Roland pointed to the nearest dune. "Split up or stay together?"

"Together, you seem nervous and defensive. I'll keep you safe."

"I am neither nervous nor defensive," Roland said.

"That is exactly what a nerv—hey, wait for me." Aignar hurried after Roland to the dune.

Roland touched the sand along the edge of the dark portal. His finger left an indentation, reminding him of a childhood trip to a beach and building a sand castle with his parents.

"The other lance should've left a multi-spectrum tag around whatever portal they went through," Roland said. "Left another tag once they came back out." He switched between optics feeds as he scanned along the edge of the portals.

"I'd say it shouldn't have taken them long to go through any of these dunes," Aignar said.

"They're a little bigger than a Mule cargo compartment. But this Qa'Resh tech…who knows what happens when you go through? Might end up on Earth in the 1990s. Get sent to some far-flung galaxy on a living ship with a misfit crew or—"

"There." Roland said and pointed to a dune farther along the circle. "Got a hit on the ultraviolet."

"We want to follow them or go our own way?" Aignar asked.

Roland got to the dune and placed his palm over a streak running perpendicular from the edge of the portal. A pale-white light lit up in his palm and a word appeared within the streak: ERREGELA.

"The mark should be the name of the lance and what time they came through," Roland said. "Who's 'erregela'?"

"Let's go ask." Aignar pointed to the portal.

"It's your turn." Roland stepped back and waved Aignar toward the pitch-black circle.

"Fine, but if we step through to some planet

where we're worshiped as god emperors, I am not sharing my palace with you." Aignar pushed his camera probes through the portal, then snapped them back as he stepped forward. "Looks boring."

Roland followed him through. The inside of the dune was far larger than the exterior. Ivory-colored passageways, all lit from within, stretched into the distance. Oval-shaped gaps in the walls gave the place a membrane-like feeling, as if they were inside something organic.

The only sound was the dull whine of their armors' actuators and the click of their gauss cannons.

"I'll mark the interior." Roland turned around and froze. Behind him was a rounded alcove…and no portal. "Problem. We have a problem."

"That's why the other lance hasn't come out," Aignar said. "Let's keep moving. Staying here and feeling sorry for ourselves won't change anything. Maybe we'll find the others, have a good laugh about all this."

One of Roland's fingers unhinged at a knuckle. He swiped a tag down the wall and marched down the passageway. Through the oval gaps in the walls, none of which were the same size or orientation as the others, Roland saw other tunnels and the occasional empty room.

"You know anything about the Qa'Resh?" Aignar asked.

"I checked their file on the *Scipio*'s computers on the trip over. Ancient race that organized the alliance against the Xaros. Lived on a city floating in a gas giant...looked like giant crystal jellyfish," Roland said.

"And they up and vanished after the war, just like the Toth," Aignar said. "No reason given. Their whole file is pretty sparse reading. Is it me, or is there an information gap about the final days of the Ember War?"

"I've noticed that too." Roland readied his gauss cannons as they passed by a gap in the wall large enough for them to step through. Beyond was an empty white room.

"Why keep it secret?" Aignar asked. "The war's over. We won. Parades, holidays…no extinction events. What's the point of hiding information about that victory?"

"Every government has secrets. Military and intelligence information is kept off the grid to keep enemies guessing. Then there are some unsavory reasons: corruption, illegal acts…something shameful or wrong that might shake the people's trust in their leaders or upset allies."

"I'd say we're getting close to tinfoil-hat territory." Aignar rapped his knuckles against his helm. "But mine is composite graphenium. Maybe we should go back to that room we just saw…that's now full of portals."

"What?" Roland turned around. Aignar was right; the white room had three dark portals on the walls.

Aignar tagged the gap between the room and the tunnel and stopped in the middle of the room.

"Your guess is as good as mine," he said. The middle portal rippled and a hazy image of the structure's surface appeared. To the left, the spinning sculpture.

Roland watched the right-most portal as shadows played across the surface.

"I'm tempted to go back up top," Aignar said. "Regroup with Gideon and see if he's got a better option than us fumbling around in the dark down here."

"Here." Roland said and motioned to the third portal. "I think I see someone. It's weak, but you can pick up the outline."

The portal showing the art chamber faded to black as the color on the image to the surface drained away.

"We should choose now," Aignar said.

Roland jumped through the third portal. He fell a few feet and found himself in a roughly spherical chamber. The walls glittering with crystals like he was inside a giant geode. In the center of the room was a woman, her arms outstretched into a golden lattice that floated around her. Her feet floated just above the ground.

She wore a simple robe and had shoulder-length black hair that glistened in the light. She had her back to him, so he couldn't make out her face. Aignar landed next to him.

"I tried to help," she said, her voice echoing off the walls. "Tried to send you home…but armor only takes in the brave and the bold."

Roland aimed his gauss cannons at her and sidestepped around the room. His HUD showed the atmosphere in the room was pure nitrogen…and cold, so cold he could almost feel a chill through his womb.

She spun around slowly, and Roland stopped dead in his tracks when he saw her face. She wore no life-support gear, in an environment that would have killed an unsuited human in minutes. Her skin had a silver sheen to it, and; her face was motionless, doll-like. Her eyes did not blink or move, but he sensed a soul behind her still gaze.

"What are you?" Roland asked. "Some sort of Qa'Resh caretaker?"

She laughed, mocking him, the sound coming through a mouth that didn't move.

"How quick they forget. All I've done for you and Earth and this is my reward. Anonymity."

"I know that face," Aignar said.

Roland studied her again, and the chill in his womb found its way to his heart.

Stacey Ibarra.

"By order of the Terran Union," Roland said, "you are hereby under arrest for treason."

"Treason? I am the only one trying to save us all, and they have the gall—the audacity—to say *I* am the traitor?" Stacey asked. "Do you know where we are? What I'm on the cusp of discovering?"

"I don't care." Roland took a step toward her.

"*Stop,*" Ibarra said. The word carried a tone of command so strong that Roland actually obeyed her. He felt his cheeks flush. He, armor, caught short by the word of an unarmed woman.

"They didn't tell you why I'm here, did

they?" she asked. "Tell you what I'm after, why it's so important. Of course, God forbid you have the chance to make your own decisions. They just let you loose."

"Why don't you enlighten us?" Aignar said.

"This is the map room," she said. "A cartography center of an ancient and powerful race…one that didn't quite clean up after itself when they decided to move on. I can find one of those toys if you two would just…let…me…finish!"

"What happened to you?" Roland let his gauss cannons angle toward the floor.

She giggled, then, the laugh growing into a cackle that came from a place not rooted in sanity. That she laughed without her chest moving bothered Roland more than anything.

"Our salvation was our destruction," she said, "and they are our salvation again. How's that coin flip going to end up? I don't know, but we're going to find out. You. Me. Earth. The whole galaxy."

"Ms. Ibarra, you don't sound well," Roland said. "Come with me. Have your fleet surrender and no one else has to get hurt."

"Is that…a threat?" She cocked her head to one side. "You think I'm afraid of you?"

"I don't want you to be afraid of me," Roland said. "I want this situation between you, your people, and Earth to end."

"Oh, this situation is about to end." She raised her chin slightly, then said in a singsong voice, "Nicodemus…time to shine."

A dark figure jumped through the portal behind Aignar and landed in a crouch. Armor, its surface painted black, looked up at Roland and Aignar. Nicodemus' helm had a pair of golden wings on the sides, and the. The front was a blank faceplate with red optics glowing in the eye slits.

Aignar swung his gauss cannons away from Stacey toward the new arrival. Nicodemus darted forward and chopped a hand across Aignar's gun arm. The gauss cannon fired, missing the Ibarran armor and tearing up the floor.

Nicodemus rammed his fingers into Aignar's helm, crushing the optics and knocking the entire helm back on the neck servos.

Roland tried to get a clear shot with his cannons, but the attacker kept Aignar in the line of fire. Roland yelled in frustration and charged toward his friend.

There was a snap of metal on metal, and a sword slashed through Aignar's waist, just below the chamber containing his womb. Aignar's armor fell into two halves. Nicodemus, wielding a Templar sword, chopped off both Aignar's arms before he even hit the ground and then raised the sword over his head.

"No!" Roland lunged forward as the Ibarran swung down.

Nicodemus stepped forward and delivered his strike to Roland's gauss cannons. Damage icons flashed across his HUD as the front half of his weapon fell to the ground, neatly severed. Roland ducked to one side to avoid a stab to the helm, and the blade caught his rotary cannons. Nicodemus twisted his sword and the cut barrels fell loose down Roland's back.

Roland pulled his right hand back into the forearm housing and punched at the other armor's chest with the spike built into his arm.

Nicodemus twisted aside and the spike managed to scrape the black paint and nothing more. He kneed Roland square in the chest, and the blow ringing through Roland's womb like the toll of a bell. The impact sent him stumbling back. The Ibarran swung his blade up and leaped at Roland.

Roland unfurled his shield and the strike bit through the shield, stopping inches over his helm. He swapped his spike for his hand and grabbed the hilt on his leg. He activated the sword and stopped around the edge of his shield as it snapped into shape. The tip struck the upper edge of Nicodemus' breastplate and tore up the front of his helm, destroying one of the optics slits and scarring the metal.

Roland released his shield off his forearm as Nicodemus tried to pull him off-balance. The shield banged across the ground right past Stacey Ibarra, who seemed to have no interest in the battle raging right in front of her.

Nicodemus brought his sword to high guard, the hilt next to his helm. Roland kept his sword pointed at the foe, high and level with his shoulder.

The Ibarran looked hard at the sword in Roland's grip, then snapped his gaze back to Roland. Roland felt anger emanating off the black knight.

Nicodemus raised his sword just over his head and stuck toward Roland's shoulder. Roland swung his lead foot back and twisted to block. The two blades clashed, and the impact slapping Roland's blade flush against his body. The Ibarran's strength was far greater than he'd anticipated.

Nicodemus reversed the grip on his sword and thrust it down, cutting through Roland's left thigh, demolishing the hydraulics and nicking his knee servo. Damage reports flashed on his HUD and Roland faltered.

The Ibarran kicked the ankle on Roland's

failing leg, knocking it out from under him. Roland fell face-first against the ground, rolled over and swung up a desperate strike. There was a flash of steel and pain burned through his wrist. His armor's right arm ended just below the elbow.

Nicodemus stomped onto Roland's shoulder, pinning him to the ground. The Ibarran flipped the sword tip toward the ground, gripped his hilt with both hands, and lifted the pommel just over his helm.

Roland swung his left arm to deflect the blow, but he knew it was useless against the full might of another armor soldier. There, with the instrument of his certain death plunging toward him, he did not feel fear, but calm.

The sword pierced through Roland's breastplate near the shoulder, emerged out the back, and bit into the floor. The strike missed his womb, and Roland knew that was no accident. Nicodemus wrenched his sword in a circle, destroying machine works in Roland's back and shoulder.

Psychosomatic pain flared through his body.

Pulsating warnings that he was dangerously close to redlining sounded in his ears and around his womb. Roland tripped his fail-safes and all input from his armor ceased. He could still see Nicodemus looming over him, still hear the wrench of failing metal.

Roland touched his shoulder, half-expecting to feel a gaping wound from all the pain he'd felt. He looked at the inside of his womb, wondering if he'd see the Ibarran's blade when it broke through to end his life.

Nicodemus stepped away, his sword pinning Roland to the ground.

"Aignar? Can you hear me?" Roland sent over the IR.

Intermittent static came over the IR, but no answer.

The Ibarran returned a moment later, holding Roland's severed arm and the sword. He tossed the hand aside, then grabbed Roland by the back of the helm and shoved the pommel into his face.

"Where did you get this?" Nicodemus asked, barely contained fury in his words. "Did you kill her for it?"

Roland kept trying to raise Aignar.

"Answer me!" Nicodemus punched Roland in the torso, rattling him within the womb.

"They gave it to me," Roland said, his words barely coming through his damaged speakers. He swallowed a mouthful of amniosis. The naked hatred from the black knight, the damage to his armor, Aignar…all made him feel utterly helpless. "Legionnaires on Oricon…a Major Aiza. He said Morrigan wanted me to have it."

"She lives?"

"I never saw her. Never spoke to her."

"No…" Nicodemus shook his head, the one remaining optic eye swaying across Roland like a pendulum. "You stole it. Took it as some war trophy, to prove yourself to the rest of the traitors. I will carve her name into your womb and send you back to them in pieces!"

"Now, now." Stacey Ibarra leaned over

Roland's helm. Up close, she looked even more alien to Roland. Her frozen features and still eyes fell into the uncanny valley, giving her an eerie quality that sent a chill down his spine.

"Aiza is one of ours," she said. "The way he fought you," she said, tapping on Nicodemus' armor, "I have a little doubt that he could kill one such as Morrigan. Do you think Mars has fallen so far from grace that they've taken to scavenging for trophies?"

She pressed a palm against his armor and heat sapped out of his womb. Frost formed against the metal where she touched him.

"Can the other one hear me?" she asked Nicodemus.

The black knight nodded.

"Good, because I only need one to answer my questions. Has Earth changed that much since I've been gone?" She cocked her head to one side. "Because out here in the void…things have changed." She lifted her other hand up. In her palm was a small golden lattice of light. She flexed her fingers slightly, fingertips prodding the lattice until it squeezed into a bright point, then transformed into a crystal that fell into her palm.

Roland shivered inside his womb as the cold grew stronger.

"And they're going to keep changing," she said. "They'll change until we all get what we want. Power. Control. Immortality—though that last one's tricky. Seems like an incredible thing until it happens to you. Do you know the other immortal?"

She lifted her hand away.

"Could you give her a message for me? Would you do that?" She looked Roland in the eye and gave the side of his helm a pat. "Tell her we immortals should not play games with each other."

She spun around and looked up at Nicodemus.

"What was that? A prisoner?" she asked. "Why…now there's an idea. Only need one to deliver the message back to the Keeper. Which one? Which one? Which one? It's like picking a kitten. I know…" She turned her head back to Roland.

Roland tried to roll over in his womb, forgetting that he was nothing but an observer while his armor was off-line.

"We take this one," she said, jumping." She jumped onto his chest and sinking into a deep squat as she looked him over. "Because if he did kill Morrigan...I'll give him to you and the others once I'm done with him."

She clapped her hands twice and looked at Nicodemus.

"I'll get the others. You rip him out."

The black knight slapped his hands against Roland's helm and crushed it into scrap.

****

Gideon watched as a shadow moved through the storm over the artifact dome. Cha'ril's armor was supine against the metal. A data line connected the two suits.

"That was fast," Cha'ril said. "The *Scipio* acknowledged your transmission a few minutes ago."

"I told you to rest," Gideon said.

A corvette came through the storm wall and flew farther away. Gideon zoomed in on the hull and saw the ship's name stenciled on the side: EBAKI.

"That wasn't one of the ships that came with us…" Cha'ril said.

Gideon looked down the ship's flight path and saw black armor emerge from a portal not hundreds of yards away. They formed a cordon around an unsuited human. One of the armor dragged a womb from its carry handle.

Metal recovery lines rolled out of the corvette's hellhole once it came to a stop over the new arrivals.

"It's the Ibarrans." Gideon's anchor popped from his heel. He pressed the diamond-tipped bit against the azure metal and activated the drill. It twisted away, failing to gain purchase. He tried again, but his anchor would not sink.

One of the Ibarran armor pointed its forearm

cannons at Gideon, but another slapped the hand down. One of the Ibarrans picked up the woman, then grabbed a recovery line and held tight as it pulled him up and into the ship.

"Is that you, Gideon?" Nicodemus asked over an open channel. He walked a few steps toward the lance commander.

"Traitor!" Gideon cycled shells into his gauss cannon.

"Still an Iron Dragoon, are you? We have one of yours," Nicodemus said. "The other's alive. Ibarra, in her grace, will leave the portal open so you can get the other. Stand down or we'll end you. And your charge still in the artifact will spend weeks in his dead armor waiting for a rescue that will never…ever…find him."

Gideon half-bent his cannon arm, but didn't aim it.

"You have the fury, Gideon. See that it doesn't cost you another lance," Nicodemus said.

"Leave him!"

As the armor ascended to the corvette

slowly. Roland's womb dangled from its grasp like a weight on a fishing line.

"Earth is weak. We will do what we must," Nicodemus said.

"I'll find you, you coward. You Judas! I will find you and make you pay for this." Gideon pointed across the expanse at the Ibarran armor.

Nicodemus grabbed the last line.

"I look forward to it. Don't think she will be so merciful the next time we cross paths."

Gideon charged forward, energy coursing through his rail cannon vanes. He could make an unanchored shot—and die when the recoil crushed his armor or knocked him over the edge and into Oricon Prime's depths. But destroying that ship would kill Roland, doom Aignar…and Cha'ril was still on the verge of redlining.

He dialed back the charge through his rail cannon and looked away as the ship broke through the shield and vanished into the storm.

His fury was gone, replaced by failure and shame.

CHAPTER 18

Armsmen snapped to attention as Admiral Lettow stepped into the brig. In a cell closed off by both bars and a force field was Petty Officer Ruiz. She sat on a cot, her wrists and ankles bound to a heavy chain. Her head hung, staring at her hands.

The *Ardennes'* chief intelligence officer, Commander Kutcher, stood up from the brig's control station.

"Get me up to speed," Lettow said.

"We found her almost by accident," Kutcher said. "There was some anomalous data in that transmission the Ibarrans sent you. We thought it was just noise from the poor connection, then we found her system ID in the data. Couldn't recover anything substantive from that first message, which chaps my ass. Took three passes through logs before we saw where she'd logged into the telemetry exchange. From there we found her hack into the *Javelin* internal comms and her messages to the rest of her sleeper agents. First couple of words are nonsense, then instructions for the artillery strike that took out the first Kesaht ship."

"What's she said to you?" Lettow asked.

"Won't answer questions. She seems disorientated, confused. Might be a counter-interrogation technique. I need to work her over for a few more hours to know for sure."

"What about the others?"

"They all surrendered after you ordered the fleet to attack." Kutcher shook his head. "Their cell was perfect. No communication between any of them as far as I can find. No co-located assignments. They're all isolated on their own ships. I'll have them brought aboard and start the interrogations. Too many people to keep a cover story straight. I'll get to the bottom of this, find out who else is working for the Ibarrans."

"There's a connection between these sleeper agents," Lettow said. "One that's…going to be difficult to accept. Did you open her naissance file?"

"The proccie data?" Kutcher almost whispered. "Why would I…oh no. I can't open that, sir, takes a flag officer to get through the privacy locks."

Lettow pressed a palm against a screen.

"Computer. Lift all restrictions on personnel naissance files for myself and Commander Kutcher. Authorization Lettow, Carter J."

"Warning," the computer chimed, "unauthorized access to naissance files carries a mandatory twenty-year prison sentence, loss of all pay and benefits, and—"

"I consent."

"All naissance file access is automatically reported to the Chief of Naval Operations for mandatory review. Decryption sequence initiated," the computer said.

"I'm an intelligence officer," Kutcher said. "There aren't many rules I have to follow. Lie? Cheat? Steal? All acceptable in the greater service of the Terran Union. But there was one rule that was pounded into me and every other secret squirrel type at training: Thou shalt not access proccie data."

"The Naissance Act was the first major piece of legislation President Garrett insisted on after the Ember War," Lettow said. "Human beings would be human beings; didn't matter if they were true born or if they came out of a procedural crèche. No distinction in law or treatment."

"The first, and last, law to pass unanimously if I remember right," Kutcher said.

The screen blinked green and a box popped up over Ruiz's file. Lettow pressed his fingertips against the box and the computer flashed a glaringly obvious warning that he'd accessed restricted data.

Lettow looked over Ruiz' history.

"She's a proccie, as I feared," the admiral said. "Came out of the tube…two days before the

Ibarras disappeared through the Ceres Crucible. Cross check naissance files with the rest of the sleeper agents, find the link."

"I'd rather get a slap on the wrists for looking at the data than find a smoking gun. The implications..."

"Aren't yours to worry about. I'm going to talk to her." Lettow left Kutcher behind and went to Ruiz's cell. The force field dissipated with a pop and a whiff of ozone. The cell door unlocked and the admiral stepped inside.

The force field came back on, the inner wall an opaque slate. Ruiz didn't bother to look up at Lettow.

"Why'd you do it?" he asked.

Ruiz's head tilted back. Her eyes were soft and unfocused.

"You know what you've done? How many lives we lost? What this means for our future with the Kesaht? I just want to know why. What the Ibarrans offered you."

"I...I had to, sir," she said quietly.

"You're not a slave. You made the choice to send instructions to your confederates. How did you think this would end for all of you? You think the Ibarrans care about you? This was a suicide mission. You had to know you'd be caught or killed in the fight you started."

"There was no 'why.' I just did it. Never bothered to consider what was happening. You don't think about breathing or your heart beating. Just happens, admiral," she looked aside for a moment, then sat up. "Admiral. I'm supposed to say something to admirals. It's hard…like an old memory."

"You're not making any sense."

"I can't trust you anymore," Ruiz said, her voice changed to a different accent, as though someone else was speaking through her. "You've…let the barbarians come to our walls and you're about to open the gate. You're too weak to do what must be done, so I will do it for you. Leave me alone, and I will do what must be done. Win what must be won. Leave me alone. Leave me…alone." Drool dripped from the corner of her mouth.

"Ruiz, who told you this?"

"She…loves me. She will save us. Ibarra will save us all." Ruiz's shoulders began twitching. A seizure spread through her body and she fell to the floor, limbs thrashing.

"Corpsman!" Lettow grabbed Ruiz and forced her onto her side. The seizure subsided, and her whole body went limp. Blood and foamy spittle flowed from her mouth. He felt for a pulse and a final flutter passed through her neck.

The admiral closed her eyes and stood up. He roared and stomped the cot, breaking it off the hinges. He clenched his hands into fists and waited for the anger to subside. A med team burst into the room seconds later.

He stepped around them and stalked back into the brig. The room was deathly silent. Kutcher and a pair of armsmen kept their gaze off the admiral.

Lettow walked up to the intelligence officer,

the look on his face conveying his question.

"We swept her for suicide implants," Kutcher said. "She's a proccie. Her procedural memory files are in a vault on Hawaii…we go through those and I bet we'll find more impulses hard-wired into her brain."

"The others?"

"All proccies. All with a naissance date within a few days of the Ibarras' disappearance," Kutcher said. "Takes nine days to make a proccie, and all the tubes were shut down not long after they left. If the sleeper agents are all from the same batch, we can contain them; won't be too many in the fleet. If they hard wired commands into all the proccies…"

"If the Ibarras could control almost every adult on Earth and the fleet with the snap of their fingers, they would've done it a long time ago. They must've altered the code in the last few batches of proccies once the Hale Treaty was signed."

"The more I think about this, the worse it

gets," Kutcher said.

Lettow looked back at the cell. A medic stood up from Ruiz and shook his head.

"Go through the entire fleet's naissance files. Find the others that might be compromised, but keep this quiet. We'll detain them all at once."

"Detain them for…"

"Treason."

****

Lettow's legs ached, one shoulder was stiff, verging on pain from the countless hours leaning against his holo tank. The *Ardennes* was in high orbit over Oricon Prime, the 14th's artillery ships and strike cruisers in formation with the flag ship. His cruisers and other ships—those still in fighting shape—trolled along the gas giant's upper atmosphere, scanning the depths for where ever the Ibarrans were hiding.

Ducking into the upper atmosphere of a planet was risky for any ship, damn near suicide if done on a gorgon of a world like Jupiter or Hades III. Oricon Prime's upper layers weren't as relatively benign as Saturn's, but it wasn't a garden spot.

What Oricon Prime did have was scale. It would take his fleet days to do a thorough search.

At least there was no way the Ibarrans would slip back through the Crucible gate. Not while he held high orbit.

"First probes are coming over the horizon," Strickland said. "No sign of the Ibarrans."

"I doubt they'd be so careless as to anchor where we could spot them that easily," Lettow said. "Stagger probe orbits. Don't give them a window to where we're not looking."

"All ready executed, sir. Just like you said earlier."

Lettow rubbed a hand over his face. How long had it been since he'd slept?

A message popped up on Lettow's screens; Kutcher with an urgent message.

"Strickland, bring me the butcher's bill," the

admiral said.

"Aye aye." He left the holo tank and went to the forward bridge to speak with the ship's XO.

Lettow opened Kutcher's call on his screens where the rest of the crew couldn't see who he was talking to. The intelligence officer had the same poker face as ever.

"Well?" Lettow asked.

"The rest of Ruiz's sleep cell are dead," Kutcher said. "Same system shut down that killed Ruiz. No one spoke to them, so I doubt there was any subliminal triggers. That all expired within five minutes of each other leads me to believe they were programmed to destroy themselves after they were activated."

Lettow swallowed hard. There was little left to be learned from dead men and women.

"You've found anything else to connect them to the Ibarrans?"

"Nothing. They may have been sleeper agents without even knowing it."

"And what about the rest of the fleet? How

many fall in that same naissance window as the cell?" Lettow asked.

"It's hard to get an exact count after the casualties from fighting the Kesaht, but at least ten more. We round them up now and we run the risk of triggering their poison pills. Medical did an autopsy on Ruiz, there's no physiological reason they could find for why she died. Tentative cause of death is stroke."

"I want full surveillance on everyone you identify. Anything you even suspect is out of the ordinary…detain them at once." Lettow scrolled down the list of names. His finger hovered over one in particular.

"You'll have more as I find it, sir," Kutcher said.

Lettow stabbed his screen and ended the call as Strickland walked over, a white-backed data slate in his hand. He glanced at the screen just as Lettow brushed his hand over the list of suspected sleeper agents and deleted it.

"Everything all right, admiral?" Strickland

asked.

"No…it's never a good day when you review casualty lists." Lettow took the slate from Strickland and his other hand went to the pistol holstered on his belt.

His operations officer was on Kutcher's list. If the theory that the Ibarras had made the procedurals from that time period into sleeper agents…why hadn't they activated Strickland? What were they waiting for?

Lettow unsnapped the holster flap; he could draw it in a split second if need be. The admiral struggled with what to do to Strickland. Remove him from the bridge? Wait until he acted out of character, then shoot him? Do nothing?

Damn the Ibarras, he thought. *This is what they want. Suspicion all around. Lack of trust will wreck a command just as badly as a missile strike.*

He read through the casualty numbers. Over four thousand confirmed dead. Two thousand still unaccounted for. Hundreds more badly wounded. Auburn City was in no shape to take in his wounded. Those that could be moved were being loaded onto the fleet's medical frigate, *Hope,* for immediate transit back to Earth.

He slapped the list against the side of the holo tank. The bridge crew went silent and glanced at him from their work stations.

"Sir?" Strickland stepped between the admiral and the crew.

"Did the Ibarras cause this?" He rapped the slate against the holo tank again. "Or did they do us a favor by destroying that battleship and forcing the Kesaht to spring their ambush too late to hurt us?"

"I doubt they were doing us any favors," Strickland said. "They've got their own agenda. No one minds when their enemies bleed each other dry."

"They'll see just how much fight we've got left soon as we find them," Lettow said.

An alert flashed through the holo tank. Lettow put his hand on his pistol as Strickland went to his station.

"Got a quantum field fluctuation…"

Strickland said.

"Earth find a way through the Crucible?"

"That's…odd. The fluctuation's not from the Crucible. It's just inside the Oricon Prime atmosphere. Redirecting probes. The *Beijing* and her group are the nearest ships."

"Alert them but don't send them just yet. Let's see what we're dealing with."

Oricon Prime rotated slowly within the holo tank. A single point pinged just over the dawn's edge on the far side of the gas giant. The first of several probes passed over the anomaly.

A window opened over the point, and video from the probe streamed in. A black whirlpool several kilometers wide spun in the clouds, twisting two color bands together.

"That's impossible," Strickland said. "From the sensor data…it looks like a worm hole formed there. But we don't have that technology anymore. The Qa'Resh disabled all the jump engines after the war."

"And yet," Lettow looked at the whirlpool,

its force already dissipating back into the clouds, "and yet our own eyes tell us differently."

The Ibarrans beat me, he thought. *They played me like a fiddle while they found whatever is it they came for and got away scot free. If we're not at war with the Kesaht now, we will be soon. Earth won't have the time or resources to hunt them down, and neither will the Kesaht.*

Lettow straightened up, then re-secured the flap on his pistol.

Strickland gave him a dour look.

"Continue the search," Lettow said. "We'll return to Earth soon as we're sure the Ibarrans are gone. I'll be in my quarters preparing a summary for my court martial."

CHAPTER 19

Aignar stood in front of a raised bench. Three individuals listened as he struggled to talk through the speaker in his throat. Two, a woman with a lined face but the bearing of a Marine sergeant, and General Laran of the Armor Corps, sat impassively. In the center, the President of the Terran Union, Garrett, looked increasingly agitated as Aignar spoke. Behind the armor soldier was a small group of officers.

Aignar's metal fingers twitched, clicking against one another.

"...and then they left with Warrant Officer Roland Shaw," Aignar said. "Lieutenant Gideon recovered my armor soon afterwards."

The woman with the lined face leaned toward the edge of the bench.

"Ibarra had no environmental gear?" Torni asked.

"No, ma'am. She was…she's not human. Somehow."

The woman looked at the president and Laran. "I doubt she was on Oricon looking for a cure to her condition."

"What happened to her?" Aignar asked.

"During the course of the Ember War, a number of humans were…altered," Torni said. "Some adjusted better than others. Stacey Ibarra suffered a rather traumatic incident. There were concerns for her sanity before they rebelled. I'm not sure if she's finally lost her mind."

"Did she say anything about the Kesaht?" General Laran asked. "Anything at all?"

"No, ma'am." Aignar shook his head and felt his prosthetic jaw sway.

"Any update on the Qa'Resh artifact?"

President Garrett asked Torni.

"It sank into Oricon Prime a few hours after the last of our armor was recovered," she said. "Admiral Lettow hasn't been able to find any trace of it since then."

The president picked up a gavel and slammed it against the bench. Data slates bounced against the bench top. He pointed the gavel at Aignar and one side of the president's face twitched. Garrett pushed his chair away from the bench and left through a door in the back of the room. Torni and General Laran followed him after an awkward pause.

Aignar turned around, his prosthetic feet dragging against the floor. Colonel Martel, Captain Sobieski, and Tongea rose from their seats.

"Sir, any update from Mars? Gideon and Cha'ril?" Aignar asked Martel.

"She's through medical," the colonel said. "No long term issues. She'll be back in her armor by the end of the day."

"And what about Roland?" Aignar asked.

"Where did they take him? What do they want with him?"

"We don't know where the Ibarras are hiding," Martel said. "But we will find them. The Corps never leaves a soldier behind."

"You left some details out," Tongea said, "about Nicodemus."

Aignar glanced back at the empty bench.

"Is he really one of us?" Aignar asked.

"We knew Nicodemus," Martel said. "Brave man. A warrior," he touched the red Templar cross on his uniform, "and deeply devoted to the Saint."

"Nicodemus had the cross on his armor," Aignar said. "I don't…I don't understand how someone who keeps to Saint Kallen could leave Earth and follow the Ibarras. I haven't stood the vigil yet, but I thought we took an oath to defend all of humanity, to be the light against the darkness."

"It's an oath to an ideal," Martel said. "Nicodemus and the others left because they decided the Ibarras carried the mantle to protect humanity."

"Why? Why would they think that?" Aignar asked.

Martel looked at Tongea and Sobieski. The two men nodded quickly.

"Aignar," Martel said, "what do you know about the Hale Treaty?"

CHAPTER 20

Tomenakai made his way up wide stairs that narrowed to golden doors at the top. He'd walked these stairs many times before, always marveling at the craftsmanship carved into each step. The journey began with the moment the Sanheel and Ixio first communicated over archaic radio waves, master sculptures from each race had carved the other, the undeniable unity of their races captured in the subtext. While Tomenakai was critical of the Sanheel artist's inability to capture the noble visage of that great Ixio scientist, he kept his criticism to himself. Such was not in the spirit of unity.

His new body was stiff, heightening the

sense of dissociation that came each time his mind transferred between husks. To be thrust into a raw body so soon after a passing close to the veil of death was normally an auspicious honor. But now...

The tale of the Kesaht peoples continued as Tomenakai and Primus Gor'thig marched higher. The First Meeting. The celebrations as their two peoples built cities on the other's planets. Images of Ixio and Sanheel were notably absent from the steps depicting the Ash Time. To imply that either side was responsible for the conflagration was not in the spirit of unity. Not that such carvings were necessary to remember this moment in Kesaht history. The irradiated wasteland beyond the grand domes was reminder enough of what happened when the Ixio and Sanheel acted of their own accord.

Gor'thig pressed closer to Tomenakai as the steps narrowed to the Great Unity. Tomenakai's cyborg body always tingled when he passed over this spot. Then the Rakka Inclusion, then a missing section as artists across the Kesaht Hegemony worked to perfect the moment of their savior's appearance, then the steps became blank. The Kesaht's future was up to those that walked this path to the birthplace of their sacred union.

Once, Tomenakai had dreamed of his deeds added to the steps…now he feared his failures would be immortalized instead.

A pair of saurian guards crossed crystalline halberds over the door. While their six limbs and body composition echoed the Sanheels' form, Tomenakai found few other similarities between the savior's guards and one of the Kesaht's founding races.

"No weapons," a guard hissed. A forked tongue flicked between sharp teeth at the Sanheel's ceremonial sword on his front hip.

"We were summoned," Gor'thig said.

"Summoned for failure," the other guard said. "Failures are not trusted in his presence."

"We cannot question his wisdom," Tomenakai said, dropping a hint to his companion.

Gor'thig unsnapped his sword belt and

handed the weapon over.

Gears turned in the walls around double doors. The gold doors slid into the walls, and a gust of air rushed over Tomenakai. The smell of rot and disease stung his nose, but he did not show any outward sign of unease. If Gor'thig, with his more developed sense of smell could keep his composure, Tomenakai would do the same. Such was the spirit of unity.

The savior was as Tomenakai always found him; working. Stasis pods filled the back section of the savior's chambers. Open pods with a cross section of the galaxy's known intelligent species were placed in a semi-circle around the savior's laboratory. A Naroosha spawn leader, little more than a pink lump of flesh with hook-tipped tentacles, floated in a null field over the lab. Robot arms performed surgery on the creature, adding cyborg components to its flesh. If the creature was in any pain, Tomenakai was unsure. Sometimes the subjects screamed while the savior worked. Sometimes they did not.

"Pathetic," the voice came from behind the laboratory. Tomenakai went to his knees and bowed his head. Gor'thig followed suit, albeit with some reluctance.

The savior ambled around the lab. His people were once called the Toth, and he had ascended to a more perfect form when his entire nervous system was installed into a tank that moved on four mechanical limbs.

"Master Bale," Tomenakai opened his hands over his knees, an old gesture of contrition, "the operation met with difficulty."

"'Difficulty?'" The Toth overlord's nerves writhed within his tank. "I warned you against underestimating the humans. Told you that wiping out a few outlying colonies and capturing a few small ships was nothing compared to what the humans are capable of. Was I somehow unclear when I described how they destroyed my home world?"

"Their evil is well known," Gor'thig said.

"And yet you thought you could defeat them

ship to ship. Soldier to soldier. How well did that work? Tell me?" Bale asked.

"We lost most of the expeditionary fleet," Gor'thig said. "Our fighter craft were inadequate, our ships too brittle, our ground forces had some success until the humans' accursed armor arrived."

"And we both suffered a corporeal dislocation," Tomenakai said.

"You were both killed!" Bale's fore limbs hammered against the floor. "If your immortalis implants hadn't functioned properly, you would both be lost to the unity forever."

"And we thank you for the gifts," Gor'thig said.

"They are a mistake for frontline commanders," Bale said. "What is the incentive to win if there is no consequence for losing?"

Tomenakai lifted his head.

"The consequences were severe. Ships lost, Ixion and Sanheel lessers dead with no hope of recovering their gene codes or soul cores. Entire broods of Rakka—"

"Fodder!" Bale shouted. "The Rakka are nothing. The lesser officers will be replaced in days. Your failure is twofold. The Terrans on Earth *know*. They know of you and they will come for us all. Are we prepared?"

Gor'thig's mouth moved before he spoke.

"The armadas are nearly complete. But if we are so clearly overmatched when the Terrans are in force—"

"Then we are not ready," Bale said. "I've worked tirelessly for so many years to prepare for this threat. Worked so hard to improve your cybernetics, build your fleets, the great work of constructing our own Crucibles…all put into peril because of your incompetence."

"While I will never question your wisdom," Tomenakai said, "please enlighten my ignorance. Why did you send us to Oricon?"

"Your second failure," Bale said. "The Ibarran faction got what they were after, didn't they?"

"We were…indisposed during the final

stages of the battle," Tomenakai said.

"Then we must assume the Ibarrans found the map to the Qa'Resh weapon. The humans once used such a device to murder every Toth but me. I am the last of my kind because of them. If the Ibarrans find another—one even stronger than the first—they will destroy every last race in the galaxy until only their false minds and weed bodies are left."

"Then we must attack," Gor'thig said. "We can capture more Ibarrans, learn where their leaders are hiding. To wait here for them to kill us all is madness."

"To burn their worlds is not enough," Bale said. "Imagine what would happen if *we* found the Qa'Resh weapon. The rest of the galaxy would rally behind the Kesaht, and they would beg to join our unity."

Tomenakai's spirits lifted. To imagine scores more species joining the Kesaht, the perfect peace that could be had by all once they submitted to the mind vise…He looked at the laboratory behind Bale, curious just how much progress Bale had made in his experiments.

"We can incorporate less sophisticated species easily enough," Bale said. "Unity with the other great powers must be built in increments. Thankfully, we are not the only ones that fear the humans," Bale said. "A plan is in motion. One in which we have a part."

"What can we do?" Tomenakai asked.

"You will return to the battle," Bale said, "but with a slight modification." Lights at the base of his tank blinked on and off.

Tomenakai felt the connection to his body fluctuate, then return with a rush that sent his teeth chattering.

"Your immortalis implants are disabled," Bale said.

Tomenakai slapped a hand to his chest and his jaw fell open. The implants marked him as a first among equals, proof that his essence was worth more to the Kesaht unity than the enormous cost of the devices. Even worse, to have his immortalis rendered useless…

"Your next death will be your last." The Toth ambled back to his laboratory. "Succeed in your next mission and I may reactivate the implants. Or not. Go to the armada and teach from the lessons of your failure. You die again and that should provide a nice incentive for the rest of the Kesaht to succeed. At least you'll be useful, alive or dead. Now get out of my sight."

CHAPTER 21

Roland drifted between waking and dreaming. He felt his amniosis slosh around him, but if it was real or just his body creating some manner of stimulus after so long locked away in the womb…he wasn't sure.

He felt a tingle at the base of his skull. There was a whine as the neural spike from his umbilical lines withdrew from his plugs. There was a pop as the umbilicals detached.

A line of light appeared around the width of his womb. Amniosis flooded out of the armored shell and Roland fell out as someone opened the front hatch and dumped him onto a cold concrete floor.

Roland lay face down, coughing as his body expelled the hyper-oxygenated fluid from his lungs and stomach. His weak eyes made out a blur of two men dragging his womb away. He tried to crawl after them, but his muscles were too weak from disuse to do more than lift a hand. He gagged as he expelled the last of the amniosis and his lungs breathed actual air for the first time in what could have been days or weeks. Time passed oddly while in the dark of the womb.

He slapped a palm into the puddle and pushed his chest off the ground. Fluid dribbled down his face and dripped onto his reflection. He looked haggard and pale. Roland squeezed his temples with one hand, trying to avert the headache that came after every extended mission in armor.

Around him was a simple cot bolted to a waist high wall, toilet…and bars. He was in a cell with a brick back wall, bars running up from the half walls connected to the cell door. He pulled himself up onto the cot and rubbed his legs.

Reengaging his body always came with pain, the feel of needle pricks after a limb fell asleep. A bottle of water and a tube of nutrient paste sat on a thin pillow.

Chill air sucked heat from the amniosis still clinging to Roland's body. His ears, fingers, and toes ached like he'd been on a snowy mountain for too long.

"Hello," a man said.

Roland sat up, startled. In the corner cell next to his was another man on a cot, this one cloaked in shadow.

"Are you real? You look real," the man asked.

"If I wasn't real, I doubt I'd feel this bad," Roland tried to unscrew the nutrient paste, but his hands and forearms couldn't manage the dexterity just yet.

"You must be armor, unless traveling around in those pods has become in vogue since I was last outside," the man said.

"I'm Roland Shaw. Iron Dragoons. Who're

you and where the hell am I?"

"Iron Dragoons aren't one of hers," he said. "My my. Here I thought you might have just pissed her off. If a Terran like you is here, then she must be busy."

"No offense, buddy," Roland's stomach rumbled, "but I'm really tired of cryptic garbage." He tried to open the nutrient paste tube again, but his fingers were too stiff.

"You're on Navarre," the man said. "Capital of the shiny new Ibarra Nation. I take it the promotional material hasn't made it to Earth yet. The marketers should be fired. You want some help with that? I can hear your tummy from here."

"Fine motor control takes a while to come back," Roland pressed the tube against his chest and took a wobbly step off the cot. He leaned against the half wall his cell shared with the other man's, breathing hard from the exertion.

The man stood up and stepped out of the shadows. At first glance, he had a patrician look of one on the tail edge of middle age. As he came closer, his face was eerily still and his eyes were as unblinking as a doll's.

Roland dropped the tube into the other cell and scrambled back, slipping in the puddle of amniosis and landing hard on his side with a plop.

"What's wrong?" the man asked.

"You're like her! Like Stacey Ibarra," Roland said.

The man unscrewed the cap from the tube and tossed it onto Roland's cot.

"No, my boy. The problem is that Stacey is far too much like me," he said. "Name's Marc Ibarra. Nice to meet you."

THE END

Roland's story continues in **The True Measure**, available now!

FROM THE AUTHOR

Richard Fox is the author of The Ember War Saga, and several other military history, thriller and space opera novels.

He lives in fabulous Las Vegas with his incredible wife and two boys, amazing children bent on anarchy.

He graduated from the United States Military Academy (West Point) much to his surprise and spent ten years on active duty in the United States Army. He deployed on two combat tours to Iraq and received the Combat Action Badge, Bronze Star and Presidential Unit Citation.

Sign up for his mailing list over at www.richardfoxauthor.com to stay up to date on new releases and get exclusive Ember War short stories. You can contact him at Richard@richardfoxauthor.com

Printed in Dunstable, United Kingdom